Sarah

The Letters and Diaries of a Courtier's Wife

1906-1936

EDITED BY

Alfred Shaughnessy

PETER OWEN · LONDON

ISBN 0 7206 0757 4

PETER OWEN PUBLISHERS
73 Kenway Road London SW5 0RE

First published in Great Britain 1989

© Alfred Shaughnessy 1989

Printed in Great Britain by WBC Bristol and Maesteg

For my mother

I should like to express my indebtedness to Mrs Fabrice Gauguier for permission to quote excerpts from the diaries of her grandmother as Lady Joan Mulholland, and to Lady Elizabeth Longman for permission to quote from the diaries of her mother as the Countess of Cavan.

A.F.

Foreword

The subject of this book is Sarah Polk Bradford, the only daughter of Judge James C. Bradford of Nashville, Tennessee, and of Sarah Polk Jones, a descendant of James Knox Polk, eleventh President of the United States. She became first Mrs Alfred Shaughnessy and later Lady Legh. Her remarkable life on both sides of the Atlantic is recorded here and described by me, her younger son, with the aid of her diaries and letters, written and received between 1906 and 1936.

Sarah's first husband and the author's father, Captain the Hon. Alfred Thomas Shaughnessy, was the younger son of Sir Thomas Shaughnessy, an Irish immigrant railroad manager, born in Milwaukee, Wisconsin, who rose from humble origins to become President of the great Canadian Pacific Railway Company and, with Waldorf Astor, the first American to take his seat in the House of Lords. When Alfred Shaughnessy was killed in 1916 serving with the Canadian forces in France, his young widow brought her three small children to England, where she witnessed the Armistice celebrations with mixed emotions but was soon caught up in the colourful life of London's post-war *haut monde*. In 1919 she met and, in 1920, married Captain the Hon. Piers Legh (nicknamed 'Joey'), Equerry, close friend and confidant to the young Prince of Wales, later King Edward VIII and finally Duke of Windsor. Thus Sarah spent much of her life at the centre of social and political affairs, counting among her close friends the Duke of Connaught and other members of the royal family, the Press lords, Northcliffe, Beaverbrook and Rothermere, as well as many political figures of the day, including Sir Philip Sassoon, Lord De La Warr, the Duff Coopers, Leo Amerys, Euan Wallaces and the Hore-Belishas.

7

While reviving some of the social atmosphere of Nashville and Montreal in the early part of the century and of London in the years following the Great War, the diaries and letters also throw some shafts of light on the characters of the young Prince of Wales and his cousin, Lord Louis Mountbatten, as young men. For Sarah's second husband, Joey Legh, accompanied the Prince and Mountbatten on a royal tour to Australia and New Zealand in 1920 and went on a succession of other tours with the Prince in HMS *Renown* and HMS *Repulse* to Canada, India, Japan, Africa, Fiji, Chile, Uruguay and Argentina.

Sarah and Joey Legh remained intimate members of King Edward VIII's circle until after the Abdication, when Legh was obliged to take leave of his boss and lifelong friend, then in exile at Schloss Enzesfeld in Austria, and return home to serve King George VI and Queen Elizabeth – and later the present Queen – as Master of the Household.

After my mother's death in 1955, a tin box was discovered in which she had preserved bundles of letters, received over the years, as a girl from her parents, as an adult from male admirers and from her two husbands. She also kept a Diary, covering the years of her widowhood from 1917 to 1920. But it was not until quite recently that I decided to decipher and collate all this material in an effort to discover what sort of person my mother really was, particularly in her younger days. Children of the social bracket in which I, my brother and my sisters grew up, tended to spend more time with nannies and governesses than living in close contact with their socially occupied parents. Thus my mother seemed to me, in those days, a somewhat remote, pampered lady who was always beautifully dressed, smelt deliciously of scent and spent a lot of her time in bed. She would be in bed with her breakfast-tray in the morning – usually discussing menus with the cook – when we called in on our way to school; and she was in bed again in the evening – resting or having her massage before dressing for dinner – when we returned from school at the end of the day.

I remember that she was always emotional on Armistice Day, an occasion we always dreaded. It was upsetting for children to see their mother in tears, although we were well aware of the cause. I also recall that often when, for a treat, we were taken to a musical comedy or pantomime and ladies appeared on the stage scantily clad, my mother would turn her head away in disapproval and emit strange little grunts of disgust. This was probably due to her American streak of puritanism, and small wonder, for the letters from her father, Judge Bradford, indicate the high moral tone of her upbringing.

It was more surprising, then, to find emerging from her letters and diaries the portrait of a woman who seems to have charmed men the world over and flirted so outrageously that she managed at times to evoke envy, jealousy and disapproval in many of those closest to her. What she plainly possessed was great social flair and an ability to shine and sparkle in a drawing-room. Without possessing any deep intellectual qualities, she could hold her own in conversation and display a degree of feminine appeal calculated to arouse passion and chivalry in men and admiration from her own sex.

From 1936, when I was twenty and lived with my mother and stepfather in St James's Palace until I married, I came to know her much better than I had before and was soon aware of her deep affection for me as my father's son and namesake. But for a young man of my age to question his mother about her behaviour and relationships during her lifetime would not have been appropriate. Thus it was only quite recently that I began to piece together the clues to her younger days, her life with my father, her wartime widowhood, her busy social life and her marriage to Joey Legh in the twenties and thirties.

I feel I know her better now than at any time when she was alive. But this is often the case when communication between parent and child is scant. It is, however, a form of compensation for that defect.

Alfred Shaughnessy

Contents

Contents

11

Illustrations

People Named in the Text

To assist the reader the following notes may be useful on persons mentioned frequently in the text by initials, nicknames or Christian names:

Agnes Madame Joly de Lotbinière, an American, married to the French Canadian landowner Alain Joly de Lotbinière of Platon, a large property in Quebec County on the Gulf of St Lawrence.

Baba Lady Alexandra Curzon, daughter of the Marquess Curzon of Kedleston. She married Major 'Fruity' Metcalfe, Equerry to the Prince of Wales from 1924.

Betty Sarah's only Shaughnessy daughter, married first to Lord Grenfell, then in turn to Major Berkeley Stafford, Rex King and Commander Derek Lawson. Now a widow.

Billy Fred Shaughnessy's elder brother and heir to the barony. A KC at the Canadian Bar.

The Boy See *The P.*

Bud Mrs Réné Redmond, sister of Fred Shaughnessy, married to his best friend in Montreal. (Fred's two other sisters were Alice, married to Wyndham Beauclerk, and Marguerite, who never married.)

Campbell Sir Campbell Stuart, a Canadian from Montreal, right-hand man to Lord Northcliffe.

Claud Lord Claud Hamilton, younger son of the Duke of Abercorn and ADC, later Equerry, to the Prince of Wales.

15

Diana Sarah's daughter and only child by Sir Piers Legh, married first to the Earl of Kimberley, then to Captain Norman Colville of Penheale Manor, Launceston, Cornwall, who died in 1974. She was High Sheriff of Cornwall in 1988.

Dorothy Mrs Barrington-Ward, wife of Lancelot Barrington-Ward, the distinguished surgeon, whose brother was Editor of *The Times.* He was later knighted.

Eddie Edward Ward, son and heir to Sir Edward Ward, Bt. One of Sarah's many suitors during her widowhood, he remained a bachelor.

Eva Dame Eva Anstruther, close friend of the widower Sir Edward Ward.

Eve The Hon. Mrs Richard Bethell, widow of Captain Bethell, who died soon after taking part in the Tutankhamun expedition to Egypt. Mother of the present Lord Westbury.

Flora The Hon. Mrs Lionel Guest, an American writer and musician, married to a brother of the 1st Lord Wimborne.

Freda Mrs Dudley Ward, close friend of the Prince of Wales, who was married to William Dudley Ward, MP for Southampton and Vice-Chamberlain to the royal household of King George V. She was divorced in 1931 and married the Marques de Casa Maury.

Freddy Either the 3rd Marquess of Dufferin and Ava, whose father, the 1st Marquess, had been Governor-General of Canada in the 1870s; or Alfred Shaughnessy, Sarah's younger son.

Joan Lady Joan Mulholland, née Byng, a daughter of the Earl of Strafford and married to Captain Andrew Mulholland, who was killed in France in the Great War. Sarah's closest woman friend and fellow war widow. She was a Lady-in-Waiting to Princess Mary and later married the Earl of Cavan.

Louise Madame Louise Edvina, the Montreal-born, internationally famous opera singer, married to Rothesay Stuart-Wortley.

Mrs Mackay A neighbour and close friend of Sarah, who lived near Pashasham Lodge, Leatherhead.

Maitland Major Maitland Kersey, a wealthy Canadian from Montreal, who was the London representative of the Canadian Pacific Railway.

Max Lord Beaverbrook, the Canadian-born proprietor of Express Newspapers.

Orian Orian Davison, a young Canadian friend of Sarah's, over in England for the war. Nursed with the VAD.

The P, the Boy, HRH, the Prince All refer to HRH the Prince of Wales, later King Edward VIII and finally Duke of Windsor.

Philip Sir Philip Sassoon. Conservative MP for Hythe, Secretary to Lloyd George, Under Secretary of State for Air, 1924-7. Owner of Trent Park, Barnet, and Port Lympne, Kent.

Ralph Ralph Lambton, a kinsman of the Earl of Durham, who worked for Lloyds Bank in Paris and entertained lavishly at his apartment in the rue Henri Moisson. A dilettante, ladies' man and well-known figure in London and Paris society.

Sheila Australian-born Lady Loughborough, later Lady Milbanke.

Tommy Sarah's elder son, Thomas Bradford Shaughnessy, a lawyer living in Montreal, married to Margot Chambers of Montreal, with three daughters.

Victor Viscount Churchill, Lord Chamberlain to King Edward VII in 1902. Chairman of the Great Western Railway Company.

Members of the Prince of Wales's staff

Dudley Commander Dudley North.

'G' General G.F. Trotter.

Godfrey Sir Godfrey Thomas.

The Old Salt, the Admiral Admiral Sir Lionel Halsey.

Wal, Ned Lieut-Colonel Edward Grigg.

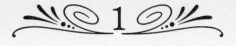

Southern Belle

Sarah Polk Bradford was born on 5 March 1891 at her parents' colonial-style mansion, Woodstock, standing amongst trees and cotton fields on the outskirts of Nashville, Tennessee. Her father, a judge, had been a member of the Nashville Bar and one of the most distinguished lawyers in the Southern states of America. As her middle name suggests, Sarah was descended from a former American president – James Knox Polk. She was also a distant relation of another president – Andrew Jackson. Her great-grandmother was a niece of Mrs Andrew Jackson and was 'the young lady of the White House' during Jackson's administration, and, like many another Southern girl, was considered one of the belles of Washington. She became the wife of General Lucius Polk, cousin of James K. Polk, eleventh President of the United States. Polk, it will be remembered, was the American president who took the United States to war against Mexico and was responsible for the annexation to the Union of the State of California.

With a brother, Thomas, one year her senior, Sarah Bradford grew up in the best society of what was in those days a modest-sized Southern town, still feeling the effects of the Civil War, in which a number of Polk men had served as officers in the Confederate Army. Apart from their estate workers in the surrounding cotton fields, Judge and Mrs Bradford kept a large indoor staff at Woodstock and little Sarah grew up in a warm and loving household of mainly Negro servants, including the nanny, butler, chauffeur, cook and others. Despite being only a generation away from total slavery, these black servants at Woodstock were completely loyal and devoted to the Bradford family and all took the keenest interest in young 'Miss Sadie' from her early childhood until the day of her wedding in 1912, which took place at Woodstock. In the days when Sarah grew up there, a bumpy, dusty road ran into town with a railroad track running alongside it. The road was called the Franklyn Pike and is still so called to this day.

Sarah at fifteen was evidently a bright child and truly loved by her parents. A letter from Judge Bradford, written from Chicago to his daughter at a boarding-school near Philadelphia in March 1906, expresses an American father's love but concern for his daughter's education in somewhat emotional and extravagant terms.

March 25th 1906

My Darling Daughter,

I have your sweet, affectionate letter and it gave me very great pleasure to receive it. I think of and love you very much and it pleases me, more than you can realize, to know that my little daughter loves me. Your Mama and I live for you and Thomas and we daily pray for your happiness . . . your report came yesterday. It is good in the main but in some studies you have not done well, particularly in Music. Here is what your teacher says: 'While touch and ear are good, they will not be really serviceable without skill. Skill, in turn, is the result of regular technical work. When Sarah has learned to discriminate between *work* and *play*, she will improve rapidly.'

Now, my daughter, do you think you are doing your full duty, when you fail to use the talents that God has given you? Don't you think you ought to apply yourself diligently and not waste your time in *play*? I do not intend to be harsh but to admonish you to make the most of your opportunities. A good education is the best thing I can give you. It is more than money. In the years ahead misfortunes may come and, if you are not equipped with a good education and a well-rounded and good character, they will crush you. I am working hard to make the money to educate you. Think of these things, my daughter, and know that your father loves you too deeply to say aught that would wound you, but that he is striving to do what he can to develop you into a cultivated,

Christian woman. I must close now. Write to me and I will write you oftener than I have done,

> Your loving father,
> James C. Bradford

The irony of that sentence about 'misfortunes to come', written only ten years before a crushing tragedy overwhelmed Sarah, has a poignancy that could not then be foreseen.

In 1906 Judge Bradford, again on a trip to Chicago, writes to Sarah in terms that suggest Polonius's advice to Laertes, for she is about to spend Easter in New York with a school-friend.

> *Hotel Metropole, Chicago*
> April 5th 1906

My Darling Daughter,

I hope you will enjoy your visit to New York. Be careful of yourself, don't take any risks and look after your health. Conduct yourself at all times amiably and politely, so that your friends may see in you the well-bred, refined and cultivated Southern girl I want my daughter to be in fact and always to appear. Your birth, station in life and rearing entitle you to a place among the best people in this country. That is why I am so anxious for you to become accomplished in Music but more than that, my dear daughter, cultivate your heart. Be kind, amiable, gentle and charitable. Above all be a Christian . . .

I am going down to Marshall Field's store to see about your dress for New York and hurry them up, so you will get it in time.

Two years later Sarah's father wrote from Paris to her finishing school at Lausanne in Switzerland. His instructions are to join her parents in Paris and travel with them to London, then by steamer from Liverpool to the United States and home to Nashville, Tennessee.

Hotel Magellan, Paris
Sept. 16th 1908

My Darling Daughter,
   You owe me a letter or two but I am not going to keep an
account with you. . . . I have engaged quarters at the St Ermine's
Hotel in London, where we will remain until we sail for home on
the 26th.

After further detailed instructions about the forthcoming
journey, Judge Bradford again reveals his concern with culture
and learning, in common with so many Americans then and now.
But, this time, he addresses his seventeen-year-old daughter in
rather more adult terms, especially on the subject of his own
increasing age and childhood memories.

. . . I have been taking strolls in nearly all quarters of Paris. Many
of my walks have been in old out-of-the-way parts of the city, not
frequented by tourists.
   We have spent the better part of three days in the Louvre . . .
examining the old Italian pictures – Filippo Lippi, Ghirlandaio,
Cimbue and others. I found myself much interested. I bought a
number of small photographs of the best paintings in the Louvre.
I was particularly charmed by the paintings of Greuze. They are
the most beautiful I ever looked at. He is modern, I suppose, and
the faces of his subjects are wonderfully pretty. I am really
beginning to love pictures. At least, if the opportunity offered,
love for Art might be developed. I feel sure I will know more of
Art next year than I do now. . . . Before I close I must tell you it is
my birthday today. I am fifty-six. That seems to be pretty old to
you, does it not? Well, it seems so to me also, although I do not
feel so horribly ancient. The years of my life cover a very eventful
period of the world's history. I was born Sept. 16th 1852 on my
father's cotton plantation in Jefferson County in the State of
Missisippi. He owned one hundred negro slaves and was, for
those times, a very rich man. He lived in a mansion that was very
much like our home, Woodstock. The planters – the class to
which our family belonged – were the aristocracy. They lived
much after the fashion of the English aristocracy. They had great

estates in land and lived in fine houses. They visited each other in great style to spend a week or a weekend. Many of them had coaches drawn by four horses. They had a passion for fine horses . . . the men hunted foxes, deer and bear and shot grouse and quail and were addicted to outdoor sports. It should also be said they played cards, bet on horse races and drank a good deal.

They settled their quarrels by the 'duello' and many a promising young man lost his life in these fatal encounters. In the Winter most of the cotton and sugar planters went to New Orleans for several weeks. They all knew each other and in that gay and brilliant American 'Paris' they indulged in social pleasures of the most elegant and refined character. New Orleans was in those days one of the most attractive cities in the world. The smaller interior towns were, many of them, extremely attractive . . . Natchez, Missisippi, near which my father and mother lived, was noted for the wealth and culture of its people. They were easy, gracious and courteous. . . . I was nine years old, when the Civil War broke out. Father had bought a cotton plantation and was living in Arkansas. The war raged for four years. I saw something of it, but I was too young to go into the Army, though I wanted to do it. The death and destruction that followed had no parallel in the world's history. The Northern Armies invaded the Country and burned and destroyed as they went. The houses of the people were plundered, then burned. When the war ended, the slaves were freed and all we had left was the land and that was mortgaged with debt. Following the war was the struggle of the Southern people to make enough to live on and lay by some. I can't tell you the scenes of those years following the War, because you wouldn't understand and it would weary you. . . . I am glad to have belonged to a race and to a people, who have suffered and achieved so much. The South is rich in all that can make a people proud and self-respecting . . . well, my dear daughter, this goes to prove that, when a man grows old, he looks backward to the scenes of his childhood and youth.

Your devoted father,
James. C. Bradford

P.S. I am writing this with a new kind of pen called a 'Stylo', which has no flexibility and does no more than stiffly make a mark.

*

In the year 1909 Judge Bradford, ever more concerned with his daughter's education and culture, sent her to a finishing school in Paris, where she made friends with a Canadian girl of her own age. This was Marguerite, eldest of the three daughters of Sir Thomas Shaughnessy, pioneer and President of the great Canadian Pacific Railway Company and one of Canada's most respected and influential men. Marguerite Shaughnessy took an instant liking to the young beauty from Tennessee with her large blue eyes and Southern drawl and when her brother, Fred, Sir Thomas's younger son, visited the establishment on a trip to Europe, Marguerite introduced him to Sarah. The pair were at once attracted to each other. Subsequently they went around Paris together and, by the winter of 1910, were what was known in those days as 'spoken for'. But Sarah, still only just nineteen, mindful of her father's strict and somewhat puritan outlook and anxious to be sure of her own feelings, persuaded Fred Shaughnessy to agree to a whole year's trial period before she would finally commit herself to him. Fred, a lusty young Canadian of twenty-one who played a lot of squash and tennis and enjoyed himself in the Montreal social whirl, found the enforced delay before marriage irksome and frustrating, for he was deeply in love and anxious to possess Sarah before someone else caught her fancy.

Early in 1911 Sarah was invited by her friend Marguerite to go to Montreal to stay with the Shaughnessys at 905 Dorchester Street. Later Sarah, anxious to return the compliment, asked her parents if she might invite Marguerite back to her home in Nashville. Judge Bradford wrote to his daughter in Montreal with his usual mixture of bland comments on nature and local news.

Feb. 12th 1911

My Darling Daughter,

It gave me much pleasure to have a letter from you. We were gratified to learn you are passing your time so pleasantly. The Canadian winter must be a very different affair from ours with all its rain, snow and mud – although the present season has been pleasant enough. There has been but little cold weather and the days have been filled with sunshine most of the time and some of the nights have been gloriously beautiful with the moon flooding the earth with light.

There has not been much gaiety since you left. We have had the Legislature since the first of the year, which is an affliction we must endure with as much patience and fortitude as we can summon to our reliefs.

You have heard that Luke Lea was elected a US Senator, which is a disgrace and a calamity. He is a moral crook and a man of no such capacity as should be sent to the Senate from Tennessee. Your mother is busy with her Art Club. They will have an exhibition of pictures, brought from all parts of the country, on the 18th. I think it will be a success and very much wish you were here to see it.

I am glad to know your friend will visit you. Don't have her come in March, if she can do so later. That month is awfully cold and disagreeable. It is the season of high winds, rain and snow. The middle of April is the best time. The weather is warmer, the air balmy and the flowers in bloom. The county is then very beautiful and you will enjoy motoring through the lanes and pikes. A trip to Hamilton Place or a picnic in the woods will be lovely.

With tenderest love,
Your devoted father,
James C. Bradford

After graduating from McGill University Fred had been working in the Canadian Pacific office at Windsor Station in Montreal. It was a job he found awkward, fearing implications of favouritism towards him as the President's son. In March, shortly before Sarah returned home to Nashville, Sir Thomas took Fred off with him on a combined business and pleasure trip to Europe. Fred wrote to Sarah from the boat.

Aboard S.S. Celtic. At Sea
March 8th 1911

. . . how difficult it was to tell you this morning of the pain and loneliness in my heart at leaving you. My love for you is so boundless and, though it would seem as though chance was against us, I cannot but feel that everything is being put in our way by Divine Providence to test our love for each other. Pray God that yours will stand the test as well as mine.

Further letters reached Sarah from Fred in Europe. One of these, from Rome, referred back to the Atlantic crossing to England in the *Celtic*.

Grand Hotel, Rome
March 24th 1911

I had such a funny experience aboard the *Celtic* which I will now describe. Among the passengers was a very pretty girl from Boston, to whom I was introduced one night at a dance on board. She was only nineteen and still at school. We became quite good friends and towards the end of the voyage she rather showed a liking for me. Well, the outcome of it all was that one night, sitting in the moonlight on the upper deck, she opened her heart to me. She said she was practically engaged to a Newark man and had promised to give him a final answer on her return from this trip. The only trouble was that she didn't love him at all times and this worried her to death, because she was afraid that she would tire of him. Imagine her confiding all this to me! Some supernatural power must have told her that, if anyone could give her advice, I was that person. I told her to make the man understand that both of them must see everything there is to be seen of life for at least a year before she would give him her answer. How I did want to help her, poor little soul. The climax was reached the last night on board, when she told me that she was going to refuse him. She said I made her forget him and begged me to write to her. She will marry him in the end, I am sure, and all will be well but better that she should wait until she is sure of herself than follow in my footsteps. Little did the poor girl know I was advising her through the medium of my own experiences . . . who can say but that I too will taste that awful bitterness of losing forever the only love I would ever cherish.

Fred's next letter came from Paris, where he was enjoying life with his father.

Hotel Meurice, Paris
April 2nd 1911

We reached here yesterday morning from gay, wicked old Monte Carlo. It was very pleasant but I feel a wreck now. On Thursday night we dined with Lord Waleran, the Chief Whip of the Conservative Party and met M. Kelposki, a friend of Dad's who used to be French Consul-General in Canada. Paris is the same old place. . . . I took a girl friend, who is staying here, to tea at Rumpelmayers but my thoughts wandered back to that day when you picked out a nice chocolate cream puff for me, do you remember, dear?

Tomorrow night we are going to the Folies Bergère and Thursday Baron Robert Rothschild has placed his box at the Opera at our disposal.

And from the Savoy Hotel in London came the first signs of unease and a touch of jealousy, for Sarah had been writing of dances, picnics and tennis parties in Nashville and jaunts to New York.

Savoy Hotel, London
April 16th

. . . it is now two weeks since I heard from you . . . is your enjoyment of pleasure driving me completely out of your thoughts? Please write to me at least once a week. What benefit can one get from a trip abroad, if there lurks continually in one's mind the horrible uncertainty of what is happening 3000 miles away.

Then on a more cheerful note:

. . . we went to *The Quaker Girl* last night, really one of the best operas I have ever seen. The music is so pretty and very well sung. I am sending you the score. Tell Marg [his sister Marguerite, now visiting Nashville, was an accomplished pianist] that I have bought one for her; as well as some pretty French waltzes which are very popular on this side. 'Les Fleurs Que Nous Aimons', also 'Tu Me Saurais Jamais', 'Valse Brune', 'Le Baiser' and a piece called 'In The Shadows'. . . . Monday we are going down to Brocket Hall to stay the weekend with Lord Mount Stephen (also of the CPR) and Tuesday to a dinner given by Lord Minto.

Soon after his return from Europe Fred Shaughnessy, still unhappy about working for the CPR as the son of the President, was beginning to think about alternative employment. He wrote to Sarah in Nashville.

905 Dorchester Street, Montreal
May 23rd 1911

. . . how would you like your husband to be a stockbroker? The senior partner in Meredith's, Canada's oldest stockbroking firm, offered me a partnership yesterday. I have not answered him yet. Had I only known that you were partial to diplomats, dear, I would long ago have entered the Civil Service. But that is impossible now . . . I intend to enter public life eventually. Picture yourself one day gracing the position of wife of the Prime Minister of Canada, which country will then be a power in the world's affairs. Rather flighty dreams of mine, are they not? But with you as Consort, one could obtain any position within the grasp of man.

All the same he was still working for the CPR when he wrote two months later to Sarah, who was visiting friends at Asheville, North Carolina.

905 Dorchester Street
July 27th 1911

. . . I have been much worried during the last two days. *The Empress of India* one of the boats I've been in charge of running on the Pacific service was held up at Quarantine with a case of Smallpox on board. This meant the detention of all the passengers on a small isolated island and they are still there. Then, to make matters worse, *The Empress of China*, outward bound, ran on a rock near Tokio, Japan and it is feared she will be a total loss. Luckily the passengers and crew were all saved . . .

there is a feeling of unrest throughout Canada, as the likelihood of a war between Germany and England grows every minute. It is to be hoped that the affair can be peacefully settled by arbitration but things are looking very black just now. Just think, dear, of my having to go out on active service just at this time, when the fondest hopes of my life are yet to be realized. And yet when England fights Canada fights too.

The war scare eventually died down, for Fred wrote to Sarah cheerfully enough that winter after she had left Montreal for New York and he was in Sir Thomas's private railroad car, *Killarney*, on his way down with his father to the family's country residence, The Fort, St Andrews, New Brunswick.

On 'Killarney'
Dec. 9th 1911

. . . I am scribbling this note on the train in pencil, as Dad and Mr. Angus are sitting in the Library, where the writing-desk is . . . how lonely I am now yet how joyously happy to have seen you again and found you the same darling Sarah who has been constantly before me in spirit for the past nine months.

Shortly before Christmas that year Fred finally decided the CPR job was no longer tenable. Being a bright young man, he had fulfilled his role in the shipping department with efficiency and industry, so much so that he was constantly being recommended for advancement. Every time his departmental head sent Fred's name up to the President's office for promotion, it was turned down. After a while Fred became impatient and decided to exercise the right granted to all employees of the CPR above a certain grade – to request an interview with Sir Thomas Shaughnessy.

Fred was duly marched into the Chief's office, armed with a prepared speech. He said it was quite plain, from the number of times he had been turned down for promotion, that his work for the company was not appreciated and for that reason he was asking the President to accept his resignation forthwith. With that Fred Shaughnessy turned on his heels and marched out, leaving his father stunned. Sir Thomas is said to have been deeply hurt and upset by his son's action and pleaded with him to reconsider. But Fred, rightly, realized that he could never be treated as an ordinary CPR employee as long as his father occupied the presidential desk.

Shortly before Christmas, 1911, Fred became a junior partner in the stockbroking firm of Meredith and Co. Then, in January 1912, after more passionate long-range correspondence, Fred and Sarah finally became officially engaged and a wedding was planned to take place in Nashville on 30 April.

In mid-January Sarah received her engagement ring from Fred and wrote to him from Woodstock in near-ecstasy.

Woodstock
Jan. 15th 1912

. . .I have been as a child with a new toy and so happy to have my first gift of betrothal in my possession . . . everybody has been so kind and affectionate . . . I have been tearing up old letters and putting others in trunks. There is a lot to do like that . . . I have decided to go up to Chicago for my trousseau instead of New York. Chicago is only a night's run (by train, of course) and Mother could accompany me but she could not be with me in New York . . . the days here are heavenly and the country is glorious. How we shall enjoy all this beauty together. Last night we had fires and Thomas and J. C. (her brother and her cousin adopted as a brother) sat for a long time in the library, talking over old times when you were here, but I became more of a dreamer than a listener.

Meanwhile, far away in Montreal, Fred began to plan the subsequent honeymoon trip to Europe.

905 Dorchester Street
Feb. 5th 1912

. . . it occurs to me you would prefer sailing from New York instead of Quebec, as that would cut out a bit of the train journey [from Nashville]. We could have a day or so in New York and then sail. What do you think? . . . tonight I have amused myself playing *our* records on the Victrola. John Macormack singing,

'I Hear You Calling' . . . if April doesn't hurry along, you will marry a shadow. I am pining away for you. Why can't people marry as soon as they first think they love each other? It seems that every day which passes is twenty-four hours of wasted happiness and life, after all, is about enough, isn't it, darling?

By 27 February the honeymoon trip to England was fixed aboard the White Star liner *Oceanic*, but on 4 March the bride-to-be in Tennessee was informed of a change of plan.

Sweetheart,

I had a letter yesterday to say the White Star has changed the schedule and the *Oceanic* is being replaced with the *Olympic*, which is a much better boat – the largest ship afloat – and easier to get lost on . . . about groomsmen, I think I could find two of my friends to come down but it means a week away from work for any man and the expense would be very heavy. Also the two railroad cars which Dad is taking down are already filled up . . . can you find some down there?

I have the steamship tickets now and the suite booked at the Savoy, also our apartment on Sherbrooke Street is fixed. . . . I am longing to take you away from Nashville when it's all over to our own little nest of love. I wonder what we will have accomplished twenty years from now, if God is good to us.

The matter of religion cropped up, oddly late in the day, when Fred next wrote to Sarah.

. . . I meant to tell you before that I am not intending to interview the Archbishop regarding our marriage. I thought you understood that when I left Nashville. You have decided that you would prefer a wedding in your own church, solemnized by your own Minister and your wishes are my commands. As you are aware, the fact of our being married by a Minister automatically excommunicates me, though I do not necessarily renounce my own [Catholic] doctrine. But we will discuss this more fully on the deck of the *Olympic*. The main thing is that I marry you or rather you marry me and that is all I care about. Let the ceremony of pronouncing us man and wife be solemnized where it may. Would you mind letting me know how many bridesmaids there are to be and whether or not you have secured the required number of ushers?

Alas, in early April, Judge Bradford suffered a stroke of paralysis and it was decided prudent to abandon the grand church wedding and settle for a quiet family ceremony in the Bradford home, Woodstock. Fred wrote:

. . . I have done nothing regarding the cancellation of our steamer accommodation and leave it entirely to you whether we will postpone our trip abroad, until Judge Bradford is better or go as originally planned, if he shows signs of improvement.

The Judge did partly regain his health and the wedding went ahead on the planned date, 30 April. From a somewhat effusive account of it in the social column of a local Nashville newspaper, it was anything but a quiet family affair, even though the actual ceremony did take place, as American weddings so often do, inside the house.

All the charm of a home wedding, all its tender associations and memories, characterized the wedding of Miss Sarah Polk Bradford and Alfred Thomas Shaughnessy of Montreal, Canada, that took place Tuesday evening at 'Woodstock', the Nashville home of Judge and Mrs James C. Bradford. This handsome old Colonial home has witnessed many a brilliant social function and many a lovely bride has left its sheltering portals but none more attractive or more lovely than the one of yesterday.

Dr Henry J. Mikell, Rector of Christ Church, performed the impressive ceremony in the presence of a brilliant and representative company of relatives and friends that had assembled from many parts of the Southern States to witness the wedding.

At the appointed hour the bridal party entered the reception room, walking between aisles made of columns of white iris, sweet peas and lilies of the valley, connected with garlands of smilax and white satin ribbons. In the front drawing-room an altar had been erected.

Palms and tall ferns formed a soft background for crystal stands of ascension lilies and lilies of the valley. Cathedral candlesticks holding white candles illuminated the scene. The bridal pair stood under a huge bell of the same white flowers. Miss Bradford was given in marriage by her father, Judge Bradford. This sweet, girlish bride, in her wedding gown of glistening white satin made on simple lines with a court train was the embodiment of sweetness and loveliness. Her veil of tulle fell in full graceful folds to the hem of her gown and was confined to her hair by a single bandeau of pearls, caught at the side with a spray of orange blossoms.

Rich rose point lace elaborately trimmed the gown. Her bouquet was a shower of lilies and maidenhair ferns. . . .

After describing in detail the apparel worn by the maid of honour and the bridesmaids, the correspondent goes on:

The fragrance of flowers will ever remain as one of the most distinct of memories connected with this wedding. Everywhere the greatest profusion, gathered from the home gardens, added their beauty to the occasion. Great Japanese vases of rare design were filled with white iris, white sweet peas, spirea and roses. Throughout the lower floor the same white and green color scheme was observed.

In the dining room the bridal party was seated at an immense round table. Overhead, the chandelier was entwined with smilax from which depended a white bell of sweet peas and snowballs. Tall silver receptacles held the same white flowers. The place favors were tiny wreaths of orange blossoms holding a gold-lettered card. Forming a brilliant circle around this central table were small tables accommodating four guests. These tables were decorated with tulips in crimson pastel shades. The mantel, sideboard and buffet were also decorated with these gorgeous blossoms. In a room across the hall small tables, also decorated with crimson tulips, seated the entire company.

*

On 4 May, after a few days in New York to recover from the wedding, Fred Shaughnessy and his bride sailed away on their European honeymoon aboard the SS *Olympic*, sister ship of another giant White Star liner then still on the stocks at the shipbuilders' yards in Belfast, later to be named *Titanic*.

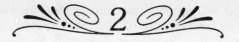

2

'Summer's Lease Hath All Too Short a Date'

Throughout the year 1912 and into 1913 Sarah and her Canadian stockbroker husband lived together in a rented apartment, No. 19 The Linton, Sherbrooke Street, Montreal – that is, if 'lived together' is the correct phrase to use. From the number of letters Sarah received during those years from Fred in Montreal, almost weekly, it is clear that they experienced long periods of separation, mostly when Sarah was with her mother, Mrs Bradford, down at Nashville. On some occasions Fred took the train South to join her, if his job at Meredith's permitted, and they did manage to spend a few weekends together during the summer at The Fort, St Andrews, New Brunswick, with the Shaughnessy family. But Fred Shaughnessy spent a lot of time alone in the apartment, or stayed late at his office or played bridge for company at the St James's Club and his letters reveal the depth of his adoration for his Southern bride, coupled with expressions of severe frustration and loneliness. Considering that my mother married my father on 30 April 1912 and that she had borne him three children by the time he was killed on 31 March 1916, I calculate that she must have been pregnant for at least two out of their four short years together. This would seem the likeliest explanation for her frequent absence from Montreal. If she often felt ill in the process of childbirth, her natural instinct would have been to run home to her mother.

Whether Sarah ever gave this as a reason for their separations to her husband is not known. But then, intimate confidences of that nature were not easily exchanged between young married couples in those days, especially between a strictly brought up Southern girl and the son of deeply religious Irish Catholic parents.

On one occasion it fell to Fred in his wife's absence to deal, somewhat ruthlessly, with a domestic upheaval in the apartment, when the cook, Kitty, had a fierce row with Watt, the maid.

19 The Linton, Sherbrooke Street
June 30th 1912

Sweetheart,

Your husband has had rather a strenuous day today. While I was out last night, it seems that Kitty and Watt had a quarrel. Kitty came into the den after I went out and turned on the light and sat down. Watt objected to this and they nearly came to blows. Well, I came in about 1 o'clock. Watt was still up. She had waited to tell me she wouldn't stay another night with Kitty, declared she was crazy and so forth. So this morning I sent for Kitty, who made counter-charges against Watt and said the maids all plotted against her. I was so sick of the whole question that I dismissed Kitty on the spot and gave Watt a sound scolding as well, because she has rather a reputation for quarrelling with the other maids. I told her if I had any more trouble with her I would dismiss her too. I was really sorry to let poor old faithful Kitty go but I think it was for the best. She is undoubtedly a hard woman to handle. I'm now trying to get another cook. Don't you pity me in my troubles?

A few weeks later Sarah was expecting her first child, and her husband, writing to her in Nashville, made a wrong assumption:

Tell me how your little one is feeling. Does he often complain of his lack of freedom. If he could realize that, safely held in your darling little body, he is further from care and worry than any mortal who has seen light, he wouldn't be so restless. Would that I could be in his place at this moment. You tell him so tonight. Tell him that, if he bothers his Madonna of a mother any more, Daddy will scold him.

*

In the event Sarah and Fred were blessed with a daughter, Betty, born in Montreal on 23 January 1913. The following April Sarah took her new baby down to Nashville to be with Mrs Bradford for a while. Fred wrote from his office to complain that the weather in Montreal was unbearably hot and sticky and:

. . . please think of me always and don't let too many men hold you in the 'turkey-trotting' position [the 'Turkey-Trot' was the new dance craze]. Or the 'Tango', which is the Latin for 'I touch'. It sends a shudder down my spine to think that erstwhile suitors can have your warm little body close against theirs with only a bit of cloth separating them from my own sacred property, while I am alone and deserted up here. How is Betty? The poor little girl won't know who her father is – she is away from him so much. And Daddy is feeling exactly the same regarding his wife.

Sarah and Betty returned to Canada in June and by the following Christmas the Fred Shaughnessys and their small daughter had given up the apartment in Sherbrooke Street and were living in a large house in fashionable Pine Avenue. Here Sarah received another of her father's long epistles, in which the Judge, his health now slightly improved, reminded his daughter of the religious meaning of Christmas. He then went on to describe the doling out of Christmas presents at Woodstock. The Judge wrote with a shaky hand in pencil, for he was still a sick man with a nurse in constant attendance.

. . . after the members of the family had been given their presents, the servants – white and black – came into the Sitting Room and their gifts were distributed. Charlie Jenkin got the most and William the next. There were, besides them two, Hattie, your mother's maid, the Cook, Dora and the two house women, Alice and Fannie; also Burford and William, the gardener – in all eight blacks. And two whites, Mrs Jessel, the housekeeper and Judkin, my nurse.

During the early part of 1914 Sarah once again left Betty in Montreal with Fred and the nurse and spent the best part of a month with her mother in New York, where Mrs Bradford was to undergo an operation. Fred wrote to his wife.

317 Pine Avenue West, Montreal
Feb. 16th 1914

. . . The weather here is terribly cold – 25 to 30 below Zero and I haven't let Betty go out yet. Mother telephones every day and has sent her a sleigh. . . . I went to a [Ice] Hockey game last night with Prince Alfred Hohenloe and won fifteen dollars on the Canadians. Bobby Howard told me he ran into you in New York at the Vanderbilt Hotel . . . be sure and tell me, as soon as you know, regarding Mrs Bradford's operation . . . it is so lonely here without you. I dined alone last night and read a book through dinner. But the worst time is later at night. I wish you were coming back soon, sweetheart. You say it does me good to miss you a bit. Darling, it shouldn't be. In our love there is no need of separation to keep the flame burning.

By early March Fred was still alone in Montreal with his small daughter, manfully coping with domestic problems and wondering whether his wife would ever return to him. Despite his intense loyalty to her under what must have been a severe strain, he allowed himself to deliver one little dart to arouse her jealousy.

317, Pine Avenue
March 7th [1914]

. . . no amount of amusement outside can offset the loneliness of this house . . . the Quinlan Opera Company is here and they are wonderful. They sing in English and are mostly Irish singers with beautiful voices. Little Felice Lyne, who you will remember created a furore in Paris last year, is with them. She is only 21 and very pretty. I supped with a lot of them at the Ritz the other night. Your hubby is right in the thick of the Opera Company. Miss Lyne is quite a friend of mine. I evidently made a great hit with her.

Satisfied with her mother's progress to recovery, Sarah soon returned from Nashville and Fred rented a small cottage at

Prout's Neck on the coast of Maine for the summer. Here Sarah and Betty were established with the nurse and the coloured maid, Hattie, loaned by Mrs Bradford from Nashville to help Sarah out. The world was still at peace and Fred, who went down most weekends to join his wife and child at the seaside, none the less wrote regularly to Sarah from Montreal during the week. His letters showed more concern with domestic matters than with world events.

St. James's Club, Montreal
June 26th 1914

. . . I hope you are very careful about Hattie's room. Don't let her have a lamp and, when she turns out the candle, tell her to be careful and keep it away from the woodwork or hangings . . . also warn her that, if ever there is a storm, be sure to close the windows in the attic. . . . I dined with Lady Allan at the Ritz last night and met there a very charming American woman, who has been staying with friends in Canada, Mrs Paul Phipps [sister of Lady Astor and mother of Joyce Grenfell]. She was a Miss Langhorne of Virginia.

But a letter reached Sarah at Prout's Neck on 24 July written in a very different mood.

. . . our stock markets here, in New York and everywhere else in the world are almost in a panic. Austria has given Servia until tomorrow to apologize for the murder of Archduke Ferdinand and, by today's indications, there is going to be a terrible European war involving Austria, Russia, France, Germany and perhaps England. You cannot realize how things are. It isn't that I am worrying over my own affairs, because luckily I am not carrying any stocks except U.S. Steel, which won't be affected. But it is all my clients' interests that demand protection. However, I am coming down on Friday and hope that I don't have to be recalled. Hohenloe is coming down with me on Aug. 14th.

The following week's letter was graver still.

Aug. 1st 1914

. . . war in Europe now seems inevitable and the stock markets all over the world are almost suspended. There were five failures in London but none here, so far, although several people are embarrassed. I don't suppose I'll get away tonight but will surely do so, unless things get worse again.

The office certainly needed me today but Mr Meredith [his employer] didn't want to disturb my holiday. We haven't reopened our exchange yet, as the situation is critical and people would sell so much that many houses would fail. But we will probably open tomorrow. Once our market opens and I know the danger is passed, I will take the first train down.

When the Great War finally broke out on 4 August Fred felt an instant need to get into it somehow. So he volunteered for part-time, home-front war service with the Canadian Militia. Sarah wrote with undue and slightly premature anxiety from Prout's Neck.

My Precious Darling,
It was hard to bring myself to believe that you would really enlist and, now that it is a positive reality, I shudder to think of the outcome of everything. I feel so helpless and despondent for, once you are in the midst, there is no backing out or doing things half-way. Therefore I had far rather know the truth and actual facts of the situation so as to prepare myself. Do not take my meaning in the wrong way for you know that I of all people would never want to see you a coward or one who shirks duty but on the other hand don't go more than half-way. I have a pang of something I can't explain when I think that it is I who is preventing you from doing something that has always been your heart's ambition. . . . I will be brave and stay here until I can stand it no longer.

As the war in Europe gathered momentum the well-to-do people of Canada, although committed to Great Britain as a dominion, did not instantly feel themselves in the firing-line, but many of them embarked on a great campaign of personal austerity. Fred reported to Sarah.

Pine Avenue
Aug. 24th 1914

. . . what will people do this winter? Prices for food will be twice what they were and there won't be any money. Dad is very depressed. Our office is closed as far as actual business is concerned, but we are busy looking after our clients. Everyone is economizing. Hartland MacDougal is shutting up his Mountain St. house and will live in the country all winter. People with motors are storing them. Some families are consolidating in one house, so as to divide expenses . . . the number of my men friends, who have either gone to the Front or are going is awful. Even George Williamson is now in England enlisting in one of the British regiments.

A few days later, as a Militiaman, Fred Shaughnessy was dispatched with thirty-two men under his command to guard the Lachine Canal and reservoir near Quebec, vital to eastern Canada's water supply. Here he experienced his first taste of active service and of the 'spy mania' already prevalent in England:

Lachine Canal
Aug. 30th 1914

. . . on three occasions we had trouble with foreigners. You see, many companies are decreasing their staffs owing to the war and a large number of these men are either German or Austrian. Once they find it impossible to leave the country and yet have no work, they are liable to start damaging things. Some fanatical German might dynamite the Canal. Hence the danger. Alfred Hohenloe was arrested the other day and all the papers in his flat were opened and read. He is having a very uncomfortable time and it is really an awkward situation for us now in his connection. He is undoubtedly active for his country in some way or another. If they find he is using his freedom here to send information abroad, he will be shot as a spy. Personally I think the poor youngster is absolutely harmless and scared to death . . . they have already taken ten prisoners on the water front. There was a report at Armoury that one chap was discovered in the grass at Lachine near the lock, acting suspiciously. The sentry challenged him but he wouldn't talk. Thinking he might be dumb, the sentry called his companion to decide what to do, whereupon the German started to run away, so of course they shot him and killed him. On examination of his clothes they found a stick of dynamite and some German letters. . . . I go on duty at seven tonight and will, of course, live in a tent until I am relieved on Wednesday. Don't worry, darling, this is only precautionary work and I will be well armed.

By September Sarah Shaughnessy, still down at Prout's Neck for the summer, was expecting her second child. Fred wrote to her.

. . . no one can ever guess at the outcome of this war and in any case the slaughter will be appalling. You won't realize until you come home to Montreal how serious it all is. The Germans are now right up to the Belgian coast and have occupied Ostend. I pray God that, before our little son arrives, the awful carnage will be over. I don't want him to open his eyes on a world of sorrow.

By the time his first son, Thomas, was born on 14 January 1915 Fred had received his commission and was on full-time war service as a captain with the Canadian 60th Battalion, training for battle at Valcartier Camp, near Quebec. Though the course was tough, the troops had some leave and some officers' wives joined their husbands for short spells, staying at a small hotel at Lake St Joseph. Not so Mrs Alfred Shaughnessy, for whose visit Fred had a better idea.

Valcartier Camp
July 6th 1915

. . . the hotel at Lake St. Joseph is rather a terrible place for children, no beach or anything and very quiet except for the military aspect, so we shall spend the three days in Quebec at the Chateau Frontenac, which will be more comfortable.

Even when Fred was finally posted overseas to England, he expected Sarah to come over too. Furthermore, he saw no reason why she should not bring their two children with her.

Valcartier Camp
Aug. 4th 1915

Darling,

Nothing will interfere with you coming over to England, you must come. It is hard enough to be away from you like this and I refuse to lose any chance of seeing you and my babies. I can get you safely settled in a place where there is no danger of airplanes and you will go on an American ship. There is no danger of any German interference with them. [After sinking the *Lusitania* on 7 May the German U-boats had been ordered to lay off US shipping.]

In November 1915 Fred's battalion was inspected by the Governor-General of Canada, HRH the Duke of Connaught [later to become a close friend of Sarah's], and all ranks were inoculated before sailing for England. Sarah remained, for the time being, at Pine Avenue with her two children.

Fred's mother-in-law, mourning the recent death of Judge Bradford, who had died the previous year, wrote to Fred on black-edged writing paper to say how proud she was that he was going off to fight for his country.

Woodstock, Nashville
Nov. 2nd 1915

My Dearest Fred,

I have just received Sarah's telegram saying you were leaving for England Friday. It makes me very sad that you have to go and I pray God to bring you back safe and sound to all those who love you . . . you are doing your duty to your country, for when she calls you must go. No man can do more than his duty. . . . I hope Sarah has decided not to go to England. There seems to be a great danger from Zeppelin raids . . . we will take good care of her here and her little ones . . . my dear Fred, I feel deeply for you and I want you to know that I love you as my own son and it has always been a great joy to me to know that Sarah's happiness is in the keeping of a man of such high character and true nobility.

But Mrs Bradford had underrated her daughter's and her son-in-law's determination to be together in England. She was also anxious about the impending arrival of Sarah's third child. For within three weeks she was writing again to Fred, now established in England – at Shorncliff Camp, near Folkestone.

Woodstock
Nov. 22nd [1915]

. . . I am so thankful to know from Sir Thomas's telegram that you arrived in safety. Sarah and the children are here with me now. She received a letter from you today and is making her preparations to leave here Tuesday week. She will go to Chicago for a few days and then on to New York. She sails for England Dec. 14th in the *New Amsterdam* . . . I was talking to her today about her return. If she is thinking of coming back in Feb. or March, she had better remain in England until she is confined and return to Canada in June. The children can then meet her and they can all go down to St. Andrews for the summer. I think the roughness of the sea might be very bad for her, considering her condition. . . . I wish you would get a position on some General's staff. You would be in much less danger. I see in the papers there is much talk of peace. I sincerely hope it may be true and you will not have to go to the Front.

On the same day Sarah wrote to her husband from Woodstock.

My darling,
Your second letter, written from the ship, came today . . . I'm glad you had a good crossing and were not sick. Life has changed, so it is hard to believe we once lived peacefully in our own home, surrounded by love. Why should you have been one of the many elected to go to this brutal war? I have grown so weak, it seems almost unbearable . . . won't you, for my sake, get a position on the Staff. Your life is too precious. And our children, the dear darlings, how I hate to part with them but I feel I am doing the right thing, coming over to be with you. I shall buy some Christmas presents in New York from both of us and have Mother give them to the children under the tree. They've both grown a lot since we've been down here.

*

Sarah arrived in England alone on Christmas Eve, 1915, and noted the following in her Diary:

Dec. 31st 1915. London I bravely started out alone to come over to Fred to be with him as much as I could before he goes to the Front and, although I didn't know if I would ever reach my destination, here I am and no end happy to be here. Fred met me at the station and we spent a glorious week in London amusing ourselves. The place was filled with soldiers, many of them having come back on leave after sixteen months fighting in the trenches.

In the New Year's Honours List of January 1916 Sir Thomas Shaughnessy was created a peer of the realm by Lloyd George for his services to Canada. Fred received the news in the Grand Hotel, Folkestone, where he and Sarah were staying together during his battalion's final training at Shorncliff Camp before going over to France.

During this time Sarah recorded in her diary her impressions of Folkestone, where she spent the days visiting the war hospitals, seeing friends in the area and occasionally, when Fred had leave, a jaunt to wartime London.

Jan. 17th 1916. Grand Hotel, Folkestone . . . London at night is now in nearly total darkness, the tops of the street lamps are painted black throwing only a shadow below, and the windows of the buildings and houses have black shades and curtains to conceal the light, while the searchlights are at work in the sky looking for Zeppelins. It is all so weird and exciting. The people, however, are very calm and don't seem to worry at all about the 'baby killers' as the Zeppelins are called.

Folkestone is a very busy and interesting place just now as it is from here that all the troops embark for France and on a clear day you can see the coast of France and hear the guns. Nearly all the Canadian troops come to Shorncliff Camp, about two miles from here, for training before going to the Front. That is why I am here. Fred is taking a two-months course but is able to live in the hotel with me. All kinds of interesting people come here. Last night the young Prince of Wales stopped in this hotel overnight on his way back to France. I know lots of people all about here and find plenty to do, visiting the hospitals etc. I can't get used to the pitiful sight of the maimed and wounded with legs and arms gone, some of them mere boys. If only the slackers were forced to do their bit instead of this unmerciful sacrifice of the flower of the Empire.

I spend a great deal of time with Lady Allan,* who has a charming place near here called Encombe in Sandgate. She has recovered wonderfully from her injuries but is simply heartbroken over the loss of her two daughters in the *Lusitania*. Martha [her surviving daughter] is nursing in a hospital here and is doing very well. Fred may be called to France next month but I hope his departure will be delayed, as I dread the time for him to go.

By a sad mischance Sarah had left Folkestone as Fred's training became intensified, and happened to be on a visit to Bath in Somerset with Lady Allan and her daughter Martha when, on 23 February, Fred's battalion was suddenly ordered to embark for France. She heard the news by telephone from someone in London.

The following day Sarah wrote to Fred.

Grand Pump Room Hotel, Bath
Feb. 26th 1916

My Darling,

I received your last two letters written in England but nothing yet from France. It's been hard not knowing where you are but suppose no news is good news. Lady A, Martha and I motored down here Tuesday in a blinding snowstorm and the weather has been cold ever since. I've wondered so often, darling, if you are suffering from the cold? Is there anything I can send you for your comfort? Bath is a very interesting old place and I am glad I came,

---

* Marguerite Allan was the wife of the Canadian shipping millionaire Sir Montagu Allan. Coming over to England in 1915 to set up a hospital for Canadian soldiers, she was aboard the *Lusitania* when the ship was torpedoed, but survived with two broken legs. Her two younger daughters, Anna and Gwen, were drowned.

for my cold is much better and with any luck, I shall shake it off altogether. Lady Holt* is here and is with us all the time. She is, of course, nice and means well but she has just about exhausted me and the others too with her never-ending conversation. It is really dreadful, as she is always the subject of her own conversation. I got another maid, leaving Marie behind, as she is a broken reed and not strong enough to be of use to me now. I have had no interesting mail since you left, except a letter from Auntie [Mrs Bradford's maiden sister in Nashville] saying the children [Betty and Tommy] were well . . . do be careful about walking out in the open. General Leckie was shot by a sniper way behind the lines. One isn't safe anywhere, it seems. We shall be here until Tuesday, then back to London. I have engaged my rooms at Bucklands Hotel for March 6th, as I am going to the Hyde Park Hotel with the Allans until Friday, when we go down to Mrs Orr-Lewis for the weekend. I am feeling very well and I want you to know I shall never regret having come over for those precious months we had together which meant so much to me and my unborn child. Do write as often as you can. I miss you but am being very brave and passing the time as best I can. Know how I love and cherish you and long to have you back again.

Your Very Own, Sarah

Their letters must have crossed, for Sarah received one from Fred, written three days before she wrote hers from Bath.

En Route
Feb. 23rd

My Darling,

This is rather a difficult task, as I am writing this note while moving over a French railroad in a cattle train! It seems like a thousand years since we said goodbye and I would be miserable beyond repair, were it not that I get some consolation knowing that each stage of the journey brings me closer to the place which I started out for. All that is necessary is for the Almighty to take

---

* Wife of Sir Herbert Holt, said to be Canada's richest man, who was a director of the Canadian Pacific Railway.

my life in His hands and bring me safely back again, which I somehow feel positive He will do. By the way, you forgot to sign that bank sheet about opening the Joint Account. You'd better go and see Mr. Oliver and tell him, if he needs my signature, to send me a new sheet. My address is: c/o 60th Canadian Bn Army Post Office, London.

An inveterate and compulsive letter-writer, Fred Shaughnessy continued to write to Sarah regularly from 'Somewhere In France'. His buoyant optimism and almost schoolboyish enthusiasm are typified by this passage from a letter, scribbled in pencil on a message pad and dated 2 March 1916, less than a month before his death:

Today is one of those days that earned France the name, 'La Belle France'. The sun is shining and the sky blue and it is just getting like summer. This morning, when I was out riding on my horse, I watched a couple of German aeroplanes attempting to escape the French anti-aircraft guns but they failed. It was wonderful to see the little white puffs of smoke all round the machines but somehow or other I felt sorry when first one, then the other shot downward and the chase was over. I suppose I haven't got hardened to things yet.

By 5 March Fred's company had been up in the line for a spell and he wrote:

. . . your husband has been only 75 yards from the Germans, in the thick of the bullets and shells for three days. We came out last night, dog-tired but really glad to have been in 'the real thing'. Of course the shells were dropping all round and the bullets were singing by at intervals but the whole thing isn't half as bad as it is painted. The company was up there for a whole night and not one man was hit. Naturally this can't go on forever. I am bound to have some casualties. Each man has about 100 to 1 chance in his favour. We go in again tomorrow night. My dug-out is small and below the ground but we have a nice fire going in it all day and night and we are fed splendidly. It is really a most interesting life.

1 Sarah Bradford on her wedding day, Nashville, Tennessee, 1912.

2 Sarah's home, Woodstock, Nashville.

3 The Hon. Marguerite Shaughnessy in the Bradfords' automobile at Woodstock, 1911.

4 Captain the Hon. Alfred Shaughnessy, 1915.

5 Lord Shaughnessy, 1918.

6 A group at Versailles in June 1919, including Captain Healy, Sarah (third from left), Joey Legh (second from left) and Ralph Lambton (centre), with Captain and Mrs Bodley (right).

Bucklands, Brook Street, Mayfair
March 8th

My own darling,

I was so glad to hear you were out of the trenches. How quickly
you went to them. I hope it will not be a regular thing just now.
To think of you actually in the midst of battle seems too strange.
Well, here I am settled into my new home, right next door to
Claridge's. I have been asked out to lunch every day but one this
week and today I lunched with Flora in a party of eight, all being
celebrated people of one kind or another. Mr. Asquith's
Secretary was one of the party and a very dull, trying person he
was too. Flora is a real curiosity, she introduced me as Lord
Shaughnessy's daughter-in-law and the future Lady S. She was
over-excited and unstrung, poor dear, and could think of nothing
better to say, I expect. I am still 'presentable' but am beginning to
feel like a ton of bricks. I received two satisfactory letters from
Woodstock about the dear children. It makes me very happy to
know they are all right. Darling, don't go looking out for German
souvenirs but, if you do happen to come upon some, it would be
interesting to have them later on. Tell me, is your batman a
success and does he make you comfortable? An officer I met
lunching the other day said so much depends on that. You see you
are always in my thoughts and I want to feel that everything is as
well as can be with you under the circumstances. I hope you have
written your father and mother, they will be anxious to hear from
you. Goodnight, my love. God bless you and keep you safe and
bring you back to me. This is my daily prayer.

All my love,
Sarah

In the Line
March 24th 1916

My Darling,

I cannot understand why my letters are not arriving with more
regularity but I suppose these things can't be helped. The snow
which fell yesterday has melted away pretty well but it is cold as
the devil. However, we are all feeling fine. This is really a most

interesting part of the line and when we move into the trenches we will be in about as exciting a part as we can go to but absolutely safe . . . all our Canadian troops are together now and we are in close touch with some of the famous British regular troops, so I believe, in this part of the line, we are going to be pretty strong. . . . God keep you always smiling 'til we next meet . . .

Your very own lover, Fred

Encombe, Sandgate,
Nr Folkestone, Kent
March 23rd

My own darling,
Folkestone is a sad spot for me now but I have enjoyed my visit here very much . . . there was a raid on Dover and Ramsgate yesterday, nine people were killed. The Canadian Hospital at Ramsgate got a bomb but nobody was hurt. I am going back to London today. Will write more when I get back 'home' to Bucklands.

Your very own, Sarah

It seems that the following letter was probably the last one Sarah wrote to her husband, since no subsequent one has been found.

Bucklands, Brook Street
March 24th 1916

My own darling,
Just a line to tell you that I am thinking of you and wishing that I could see you. I was looking over some of your old clothes tonight, and felt quite lonesome. You have been in France a month now, and I hope the next two will fly by bringing you back to me well and happy, then I hope to have something to show you and give you. Do you know we have never thought of a name for the new arrival. Do send me a few suggestions, so I can think about it too. If it is a little soldier, of course I want him called after his brave hero daddy. I saw Major Anderson today at Rumplemayer's, but did not speak to him. I think his wife was

with him. I heard today at lunch that all the Canadians were going to be moved and with the Guards (English) were going to make an attack. Is this true – say 'yes' if so. This is a short letter will write more tomorrow.

With all my love and God bless you,

Your own
Sarah

P.S. Do you receive the magazines I send?

In his letter of the following day to Sarah, from a rest area out of the line, Fred shows his concern in spite of his grim surroundings for family matters of inheritance. Marion, the wife of his elder brother, Billy, heir to the Shaughnessy barony, had just given birth to a second daughter, which prompted Fred to write: '. . . the only thing now is for us to have a boy in May [they had one son already] and then the climax will be reached'.

At the same time Fred wrote affectionately but in a cynical mood to his brother Billy, on 25 March, for Lord Shaughnessy had been making public speeches in Montreal, accusing some Canadian men of being 'slackers' by not enlisting in sufficient numbers.

. . . I have read great accounts of Dad's speech in which he criticised the recruiting. There is a whole lot in what he said but everyone out here is joking me about having lost any chance of ever getting a 'bomb-proof' job as a reward for being scared to death. It looks as though I will peg out as a poor lonely company commander, unless the war soon finishes. However, in the words of the poet, 'We should worry'. Well, Bill, I am about to start off for church, so I must close. I have been a better Catholic since coming out here than I ever was in my life before . . . this game makes one think.

The same day he wrote to Sarah, his mind still on family matters.

. . . we were inspected recently by Sir Douglas Haig. He is a fine type of man and seemed very pleased with us. . . . Bud [Fred's sister, whose husband Rene Redmond was in the trenches with him] told Rene in a letter that the family regarded our little boy as the future Baron and Marion is quite sore and disappointed.

Fred's last letter to Sarah was dated 28 March, three days before he was killed, on 31 March 1916:

. . . just back from an inspection tour of new trenches which we are going into tonight. They are pretty good . . . the magazines come all right and are a great treat . . . this is a very short letter but we are rushed to death today. When I get settled in my dug-out, I will write a much longer one.

On 2 April 1916 Sarah received the dreaded War Office telegram, and eight days after that a letter came from Major Pavey, Medical Officer to the 60th Canadian Battalion:

. . . we are all shocked at the loss of our dear brother officer, Fred. He was wounded by a shrapnel bullet close to the left shoulder blade. The bullet penetrated the heart and the end was peaceful and quiet. Poor Fred lost consciousness almost immediately. Everything possible was done. We have lost our most popular officer and all ranks mourn his death.

The Canadian newspapers carried banner headlines announcing the death in action of Lord Shaughnessy's second son and Sarah remained, seven month's pregnant, at Bucklands Hotel in Brook Street, Mayfair, to await the birth of her third child. She was inundated by letters of sympathy from both sides of the Atlantic.

War Widow

Although the death in action of young Canadians was all too frequent in 1916, Fred Shaughnessy's death seems to have shocked and saddened many people in Canada. Every newspaper in the country carried large headlines, pictures and comment on the fact that Lord Shaughnessy's extremely popular younger son had made 'the supreme sacrifice', leaving behind a 'sweet wife and two small children'. And they concluded: 'He had everything to live for.' While Sarah was still at Bucklands Hotel in London, shattered by the news, Lord and Lady Shaughnessy received messages of sympathy from the Canadian Government, the Governor-General and many hundreds of public figures, friends and admirers throughout the dominion as well as Great Britain and the United States. One charming tribute was received by Lord Shaughnessy from the Mayor of Medicine Hat in the Province of Alberta, a key station on the great CPR rail link to the West Coast: 'The heartfelt sympathies of the citizens of Medicine Hat go out to Lady Shaughnessy, your Lordship and the young wife and children at the supreme sacrifice of your gallant son.'

Only one contentious but well-meaning note was struck, in the *Montreal Witness* of 4 April 1916. Lord Shaughnessy, after initially speaking out publicly about recruiting and urging every able-bodied Canadian to join the colours, had recently made a speech unexpectedly opposing the unrestricted recruiting of every man in the country to the forces, and this had caused some criticism of the Canadian Pacific President. The article continued:

What Lord Shaughnessy said in effect was that it was a mistake to go on organizing new battalion after new battalion, when it would need as many men as Canada could spare from industrial and agricultural enterprise to fill the ranks of the battalions already authorized, and that there were already enlisted in Canada more men than he saw any means of getting transported to Great Britain inside of the next fourteen months. Many who did not read his speech but simply heard of it, got an impression that it was unpatriotic and that Lord Shaughnessy was considering more the financial welfare of his own company than the need of winning the war. So well advised, however, was Lord Shaughnessy's speech that the Government immediately saw the need of acting in accordance with it and has already stopped the formation of new battalions. Today the whole country is sympathizing with Lord Shaughnessy on the death of his younger son, who was killed while leading his men into battle 'somewhere in France'.

His Lordship's note on the death of his son and his desire that his example will inspire others to enlist, which appears elsewhere in this newspaper, will disabuse those who mistook the tenor of his remarks through misinformation.

Soon after hearing the tragic news, Lord and Lady Shaughnessy embarked at once in their private railroad car and travelled down to Nashville, Tennessee, to see their two grandchildren and to commiserate with Mrs Bradford on Fred's death. From there Lady Shaughnessy wrote to Sarah.

Woodstock, Nashville
April 10th 1916

. . . you will think it strange writing from here but having spent the day with the children I thought I would tell you how happy and well they are. Betty is so sweet and the boy is walking all around, so pleased with himself . . . the thought of our dear one giving his life for Empire and the civilized world should be consolation to us and something for his dear children to be proud of but – oh, 'what a sacrifice'. The sorrow will keep possession of us, until Providence and time will make a cure.

*

As soon as they returned to Montreal, Lord Shaughnessy wrote to Sarah a long, compassionate letter, urging her to face the future with courage.

> 905 Dorchester Street
> April 14th 1916

. . . in all the war the enemy will not take the life of a finer boy from every standpoint than dear Fred . . . it is my plan to go to England in May, if I can get a steamer, and while there, we can discuss your future plans . . . it would be nice if you could come to St Andrews with the children for the summer but the ocean situation is just now very much in the clouds . . . we must watch the progress of events and be governed accordingly . . . with worlds of love from your affectionate Daddy-in-law,

> Shaughnessy

Among the hundreds of letters Sarah received from personal friends in London and Montreal, as well as glowing tributes from Fred's brother officers, was one from Lady Drummond, like Sarah an American woman married to a Canadian.

> 208 Drummond Street, Montreal
> April 3rd 1916

Dearest Sarah,
What can I say to you? . . . I cannot make myself believe that dear, brave, funny, loveable Fred has been the first of the gallant 60th to be called to the Heaven that is now so wonderful because it holds the flower of our youth . . . I was in New York yesterday when I heard the tragic news and I felt that I could not stay among neutral Americans, that, although they were my people, I must get back here to the people who fully understand the burden of Empire that we American women who allied ourselves to Britishers have taken on . . . lovingly and heartbrokenly,

> Your friend,
> May Drummond

Another letter came for Sarah on the same day from an officer at Canadian Army Corps HQ in France, who survived the war and later fell in love with her.

GHQ Canadian Army Corps
April 3rd 1916

Dear Mrs. Shaughnessy,

I want to let you know how deeply I sympathize with you and how much I personally feel Freddie's death . . . it is not a sacrifice that will be without fruit, for he gave up so much that his influence will always be felt in the history of Canada. For him we cannot be sorry but for ourselves and especially for you we feel the keenest sorrow . . . if I can be of any service to you, please command me.

Very sincerely yours,
Talbot Lapineau

And from a former housemaid, who had worked for Fred and Sarah at Pine Avenue:

697 St. Joseph's Street, Lachine
P of Quebec
April 8th 1916

Dear Mrs. Shaughnessy,

Please accept my deepest sympathy in your sad loss. Words are but poor at such a time but I pray God may give you strength to bear it for the dear children's sake. The Captain would not wish you to grieve too much, as he died fighting for his country, a brave and gallant soldier. I shall always have the memory of a kind master with a smile and a pleasant word at all times. If there is anything I can do for you, the above address will always find me. Trusting you have a safe journey home with your new baby, allow me to remain,

Yours Sincerely,
Emily Winch

As soon as her new baby, Alfred James, born on 19 May, had been christened at the Catholic Church of St James's, Spanish

Place, off Manchester Square in London, Sarah embarked for the United States with her son and his nurse in the White Star liner SS *Olympic*, the very same ship on which she and Fred had set sail almost exactly four years earlier on their honeymoon trip to Europe.

Once back in America, she went to Nashville to see her mother and collect the other two children for transportation to Montreal. What happened next is not totally clear, but there can be little doubt that Sarah took her children down to St Andrews for the rest of the summer of 1916, where, to the distress and surprise of Lord and Lady Shaughnessy, she announced her intention of buying a house in London and making her future home in England. Whether this plan was supported financially by Lord Shaughnessy or by her own mother, Mrs Bradford, is not known. Fred Shaughnessy's modest estate was under probate, but a trust was to be formed for his children.

Whatever Sarah's father-in-law thought about her decision, there can be no doubt of Lady Shaughnessy's bitter anger and disappointment. Nevertheless the autumn of 1917 found Sarah resident in London with her three Shaughnessy children and a small staff of servants at 51 Sussex Gardens, W2, a large, tall terrace house close to Paddington Station.

In late October she was staying with a friend at a house called Lingwood in Cobham, near Leatherhead. While there she may well have looked around for a possible country residence for herself. At this address in Surrey a letter arrived for Sarah from Talbot Lapineau, the French Canadian staff officer at Corps HQ who had written to her on Fred's death and with whom she had in the interval evidently become friendly.

> *Hotel Jules, Jermyn Street*
> Oct. 15th 1917

My Dear Sarah,
I have missed you. I miss you. I would like to hear you play *Bohème* again tonight. I shall never forget how you played and how you looked. No real sight of 'craterland' will dull that memory from my inward eye. I am dashing this off before dinner. . . . I saw Martha [Allan] for tea at the Carlton and we had

a pleasant chat. Out of nothing Martha said, 'I didn't know you were so fond of Sarah.' I replied, 'Of course. I have always been, just as I have always been fond of Alison.' And left it at that. I shall not be responsible for more than that publicly. So whatever gossip may carry to your ears, hold me guiltless! I suppose we cannot live without a certain undercurrent of talk. Charlie already teases me and I grow furious. He told me that Lord Beaverbrook was much attracted to you and I fumed and stormed quite naturally and sincerely until I calmed myself . . . give my love to Betty and Tommy . . . they say there will be more air raids next week, so stay where you are . . . I wish the future was not so uncertain. I have nothing certain to depend upon, not even you.

Affectionately,
Talbot

In early November Sarah received a telegram at her London house from her brother, Thomas Bradford, who was attending an artillery course at Fontainebleau near Paris before being drafted to an American unit at the Front. He had been granted four days' leave and urged his sister to join him in Paris, if she could manage to wangle a passage across the Channel. But crossing the Channel in wartime presented problems, so Sarah promptly telephoned a friend, Sir Charles Gordon, a wealthy and influential Canadian, who happened to be in London. Gordon arranged for her to travel to Paris on 24 November with the Allied Mission. She wrote afterwards in her Diary:

Dec. 1917 I was invited to go with the Prime Minister, Mr. Lloyd George, and all the members of the great Allied Conference that was to be held in Paris. It was the most important gathering of the 'Entente' powers since the beginning of the war.

Lady Northcliffe and I were the only women in the party and I found her a most delightful companion.

We travelled by special train from London to Dover, where we boarded a sort of Channel war cruiser in the most military fashion and were escorted across by five torpedo boat destroyers. Calais presented more than anywhere else a war aspect and every building had its camouflage. Our special train was soon off to Paris. What struck me most forcibly was the desolation and the thousands of Chinese Coolie Labour Battalions working behind the lines.

I must say they looked odd and terrified with the dreary background of cemeteries and inches of mud and slush. En route we passed through Amiens, Abbeville and Etaples, which at one time, in the early days of the war, was invaded by the Germans. One saw hospitals from afar but more predominantly YMCA huts and WAACS.

Mr. Lloyd George invited Lord and Lady Northcliffe and myself to lunch with him in the train. Just the four of us. I was, of course, thrilled and shall always remember the interesting history-making conversation and how little the public knows of what is going on. Lloyd George is a most charming person to meet and impressed me with his keenness, extraordinary vitality and quick wit.

He and Lord Northcliffe talked very freely about the war and the Conference, also what America meant to the Allies in this struggle. I was greatly gratified to hear America given her just due by the two most powerful men in the Empire!

One feels that a thorough understanding now exists between America and England and it will increase daily as time goes on. Lord Northcliffe has certainly done much to bring about this feeling.

The Prime Minister expressed to me keen interest in the Southern States of America and said he hoped to know them some day. Lord Reading joined us after and discussed the post of Ambassador to the USA, which I see he has since accepted. During the journey I also met Mr. A. J. Balfour, Sir William Robertson, the Chief of Staff, Lords Milner, Newton [later to become her father-in-law], Sir Eric Geddes, First Lord of the Admiralty, Sir John Jellicoe, General Sir Henry Wilson, General Sykes, M. Venizelos, the Greek Prime Minister and others.

On our arrival in Paris we were met by M. Clemenceau. It was a wonderful trip. Mr. Lloyd George asked me to return with him the following Monday but I was staying on in Paris longer, so returned home later via Le Havre with Louise Edvina [the Montreal-born operatic soprano, who was a close friend].

✻

Before her trip to Paris Sarah had rented a country house near Leatherhead in Surrey, called Pashasham Lodge, for weekends and holidays. She soon decided to make Leatherhead her main home.

Jan. 11th 1918 Am up in London for a few days from Leatherhead to try and let 51, Sussex Gardens, since the air raids seem to get worse instead of better. The Duke of Connaught [a son of Queen Victoria and uncle of King George V] telephoned to say he would like to come to tea with me. I told him the house was in curl papers but he insisted, so I gave him tea in a corner of the drawing room, which was completely dismantled, no furniture, just dust-sheets, and packing cases. He said one didn't mind about trifles now. What queer things we do in wartime!

Jan. 14th Today is Tommy's birthday. Three years old.

Jan. 15th Dined with Flora Guest [The Hon. Mrs Lionel Guest, an American and lifelong friend] and met Mr. Balfour. A charming, delightful man of the old school. He told us much of his American mission, which he enjoyed and appreciated. Sir Arthur Steel Maitland, M.P. and Lady Drummond were the others there.

Jan. 20th Dined with Flora Guest and sat next to Stephen McKenna, author of *Sonia*. A strange and peculiar man. He tried to convince me there was no God – but with little success. Also there was Elizabeth Asquith [later Princess Antoine Bibesco] wonderfully clever and attractive but won't let you forget it. She thinks so too. The other people made no impression.

Jan. 23rd Today is Betty's [her daughter's] birthday. Five years old. I had a party for her and Tommy [her elder son, then aged three]. Each had their separate cakes and candles. War cakes, of course, with no icing or decorations. Bud's baby, Margot, spent the day here and the Harding children came to tea. They had a lovely time and I was most happy.

Jan. 25th Came up to London to see about letting Sussex

Gardens, which has been empty for so long. Hope I can make a proper agreement, as the expense of two houses is too much for me. Lunched with Lord and Lady Edward Gleichen and met General Geoffrey Glyn, who seemed natural and frank and enjoyed a laugh. It was a meatless, butterless meal and things will get worse later on. Dined at home. Got an air raid warning at 11.30 but nothing happened.

Jan. 28th Back at Pashasham Lodge. The weather is warm and balmy. Am feeling worried about my next move. Do hope to keep on the country house, as I don't want to take the children back to London on account of the air raids. It is so nice having my friends to stay, otherwise the loneliness is appalling. Betty and I worked in the garden, brushed up leaves etc. We have no gardener now. Played with children from tea time on. Domestic troubles are most worrying. Cook gave notice to marry a soldier. No luck. Food ration cards came and we soon begin the use of tickets. All butchers' shops closed except for three days in the week. And no butter whatever. I think things are very serious. One feels very hungry. Big air raid on London last night. Guns could be heard down here.

Jan. 29th Heavenly warm, sunny day. Took Tommy and Freddy for a walk in the morning and Betty to her dancing lessons in afternoon. Was feeling very depressed today but soon got myself in hand.

Jan. 31st Flora and Lionel Guest arrived after tea to stay until Monday. I love having them. Flora brings so much life and joyfulness into the house.

Feb. 2nd Jack Todd has arrived from Canada and came down for lunch today. Told me all the Montreal news, which made things seem so distant. Nothing interested me very much and I felt glad that I am where I am, with never one single regret of having come to England. Jack says Lord Shaughnessy is very blind but, after the operation, he will be all right.

Feb. 3rd Sir Edward Ward and Dame Eva Anstruther came

down to lunch. First visit here. The day was very pleasant. The children came in after lunch and behaved very well. Flora and Lionel left this afternoon and later on I walked half way to the station with Sir Edward and Eva. I miss my friends and the house seems very empty and lonely.

Feb. 4th Spent a quiet day alone. Went for a walk with the children and read *Jeanne Christophe*. Weather very Spring like.

Feb. 5th Came up to London this morning, staying at my house, which is not yet let. Lunched at Ritz with Louise Edvina, who leaves for Paris on Friday to take up her singing again. Commander Brind came to tea and unfolded his wonderful scheme for the Air Service and I promised to arrange for him to meet Lord Rothermere, Minister of the Air Board, through Sir Campbell Stuart. Dined at Junior Army and Navy Club with Eddie.

Feb. 7th I transacted some business about my house this morning and lunched with Flora Guest. Met at lunch J.H. Thomas, M.P. and Arthur Henderson, Secretary of the Labour Party. Both most interesting 'men of the people' – dropped their 'H's' but very clever. They discussed freely the Labour Question and their Peace Terms. Thomas said England was this week on the verge of a revolution, there was terrific unrest among the people. I don't believe this. England is not the country for revolution! J.H. Thomas, who went to America, said [President] Wilson is not a great man; that he has chosen second-rate politicians for his Cabinet, so that he will be all-powerful; also that he considered England more democratic than America today. I didn't agree but different points of view are interesting.

Feb. 9th In morning Flora and I went over Library for Soldiers on all Fronts, run by Sir Edward. Lunched after with Dame Eva, whom I like enormously. Brilliant woman.

Feb. 12th Came up to London again today to go with Sir Edward Ward to the Opening of Parliament by the King. The ceremony was interesting, seeing the Prime Minister and all the

M.P.s going into the House of Lords. When it was all over the King and Queen got very little cheering.

Feb. 18th Bad air raid on London last night. 60 killed. We heard the guns and barrage from here. The crocuses and primroses are in bloom. They give a breath of spring.

Feb. 19th Came to London for day to put house in order, as it is at last let – for two months to a Mrs Horniman. Trott [her lady's maid] and I have been working hard all day, emptying cupboards etc.

Feb. 24th Played golf with Mrs Mackay in pouring rain. Lady Beaverbrook and Lady Holt came over from Cherkley to tea.

Feb. 27th Came up to stay for a few days in London with Lady Joan Mulholland [who, also widowed in the war, became her closest woman friend for many years] and met at tea Lord Claud Hamilton, who is ADC to the Prince of Wales. Dined at Claridge's and went to the play, *Billetted*. Joan is such a darling.

Feb. 28th Lord Queenborough and Lieut. Cunningham-Reid came to dinner. Joan and I talked very late.

March 1st Joan and I lunched with Maitland Kersey [a wealthy Canadian living in London] at Claridge's. He gave us his motor for the afternoon and we went to see a clairvoyant at 190a, Notting Hill Gate. I spent an hour with her. She was very good but I came away feeling depressed.

March 5th My birthday. 27 years old. Came to London to stay with Joan. Lunched with Jack Todd and the President of Alberta University at Ritz. Afterwards went with Jack to see war pictures at Grafton Galleries. We dined at home early, went to hear *Faust* with Mr Philip Gardner of the Foreign Office and Capt. Harding in Lord Queenborough's box. Opera was lovely.

March 7th Joan and I dined at Claridge's and went to see *Yes, Uncle* with Maitland [Kersey] and Commander Sir Douglas

Brownrigg. Back to Maitland's house for supper. Just as we got in, the guns started and the raid lasted until one o'clock in the morning. The noise was terrific but I was very calm. It was the first raid I've been in.

March 21st Stayed up in London with Joan. Lord Hugh Grosvenor and Lady Airlie there. The great German offensive has started today. Dined at Claridge's with Agnes and Alain [de Lotbinière]. Terrible news of German bombardment of Paris. Agnes' children are there. We are doing everything to get news through. Lord Beaverbrook is a great help. He came over to see me this afternoon.

March 25th Came to London early to be with Agnes at Bucklands Hotel. Still trying to get news. Lunched at Claridge's and on to Club for Overseas Women, which Queen Mary visited. Was presented to her. Dined with Agnes and Sir George Noble and went to see *Dear Brutus*.

March 27th Went to Opera with nice Lady Ulrica Baring and a Mr. Gibbons to hear *Tannhauser*. Found it rather long.

March 28th Agnes, Alain and I came home in the afternoon to the country. A man nearly died in our railway carriage. We had to take him home in our taxi. My new lady gardener has arrived and is busy digging. She is a Miss Amos and I like her very much. She is 23, strong and capable.

March 29th Went to London to spend night with Agnes at Bucklands. Alain left for Paris today but no women are allowed to travel, since the great offensive started.

Poor Agnes, she is so worried about her children, who are in Paris, as there are grave fears that the Huns may break through to Paris and Calais. We have had a very quiet day.

March 30th Agnes and I returned to country this afternoon. We went over to Cherkley to dine with Lord and Lady Beaverbrook. Lord B. was very pessimistic about the way the war is going. He said the Fall of Babylon was mild in comparison with this present battle and the slaughter. He said Haig and Gough should be sacked and that America had been a great disappointment. After dinner we saw some wonderful films.

March 31st Easter Sunday. Today, two years ago, Fred was killed in France. The day has been trying and sad but I've felt a wonderful peace in the knowledge that he is happy and out of this terrible war.

April 1st We were all busy working in the garden, planting seeds and vegetables. The children have four rabbits, which Flora Guest gave them and two escaped from their hatch but were recaptured.

April 4th A quiet, lovely sunny day. Agnes, by special permission, went to Paris via Boulogne. Very sad to have her go but she was not happy here with her children over there. What terrible times these are!

April 5th Went to London to say goodbye to Eddie [Ward], who goes to Cambridge on a Staff Course. We lunched and went to the Hippodrome and dined at the Savoy. There is a new regulation now that all lights must be out by 10.30 pm in hotels and restaurants. Not a bad thing either. Why didn't we think of that three years ago?

April 8th Betty and I weeded the flower beds all morning. Miss Amos, Horace and I chased a rabbit, which escaped for one hour into the bushes, but with no luck. After lunch I helped Miss Amos dig up an old turnip patch. Was so tired after my labours I retired to bed before dinner and Trott washed my hair.

April 10th Rainy day. Betty and I went into Oxshott to buy some more hens from Mr. Taylor. I wrote all afternoon and read in the evening. Retired early.

April 12th Went to London to spend night with Joan. Everybody is very depressed about the steady advance of the Germans. General Gough seems to be in disgrace over retreat of the 6th Army. Dined at Savoy with Lady Manton, Capt. Cecil Harding and Capt. Antrobus. All lights are out at 10.30, so we retired early.

April 13th Felt miserable with bad cold. Lady Drogheda's dance in Holy Week and during this critical battle has made her most unpopular. The King spoke to her about it. It was a terrible thing to do and I'm glad she was called down. A heartless thing.

April 14th Caught train to Shoreham to stay with Orian Davidson and Clara Scott. Shoreham is a very ugly place. Weather so bad we didn't venture out until this afternoon, when Clara and I motored into Brighton to shop. I bought the children some gramophone records.

April 16th Returned home to find snow on the ground in Surrey. Winter has come. Children love the records. Retired early to bed and am reading *The Green Mirror*.

April 17th Cold still bad. Miserable rainy day. Germans are still advancing. Paris is bombarded every day. Had a letter from Agnes, who is there. Says it's hellish.

April 19th Went with Sir Edward and Dame Eva Anstruther up to Cambridge to see Eddie. We had rooms at the Bull Hotel. Eddie looks splendid and thinner. He came to dinner and stayed until ten.

April 20th Eva and I explored Cambridge, visiting the antique shops, where I bought an old chair quite cheaply. In the afternoon Sir Edward took us to tea with his friend, Dr. James, Head of King's College. He is most interesting, a recluse, and writes ghost stories [M.R. James]. Dr. James took us through King's Chapel and explained all the points of interest. To my mind, it is the most perfect gem of a church I have seen anywhere and I've seen a lot. I love being here and we are enjoying every minute of it.

April 21st Went for a walk this morning with Eddie. Bitterly cold weather. Capt. Janson and his wife lunched with us. Very dull, nondescript people. After lunch we all went over to Eddie's rooms in Clare College. Received letter this morning from Thomas [her brother] saying he was all right. I feel relieved. First news of him in six weeks. Returned to London.

April 23rd Lunched with Dorothy Barrington-Ward [great friend and wife of Lancelot B-W, the distinguished surgeon], and dined at Ritz with Jerry Farrell [from Montreal]. Large dinner for 20. Jerry gave me lots of Montreal news, which interested me but little.

April 24th Ran into Billy Shaughnessy [her brother-in-law] at the Carlton. He came down in the afternoon to Pashasham to see children. We showed him the little farm, rabbits, chickens etc. Very bad storm but later I heard the first cuckoo.

April 26th Joan told me a secret today, that she had been asked to be Lady-in-Waiting to Princess Mary. We came down together yesterday to stay at Kyson, Woodbridge, Suffolk with Maitland Kersey. After lunch we motored over to the Martlesham aerodrome and watched the flying and from there to Bordsey, a lovely place on the sea, where we distinctly heard the guns in France.

April 29th Came home this morning. Betty's first tooth came out and she is thrilled. One best hen has died and I feel very sad and discouraged. Do hope they won't all pass away. We think it is the food we buy. Am tired and depressed tonight.

Am reading a book called, *Bones and I* by Whyte-Melville. Like it very much.

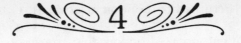

The Turn of the Tide

Throughout the summer of 1918, as the war still raged on the Western Front, Sarah Shaughnessy divided her time between Leatherhead and London. Travelling up by train from Pashasham Lodge sometimes for the day, often staying up for the night at Sussex Gardens, when it was not let, or with friends or at hotels when it was, she continued to pursue her social life, lunching and dining in private houses, as well as at the Ritz, the Berkeley, the Carlton and Claridge's, meeting old friends from the United States and Canada and making new English ones. She worked intermittently in the US Canteen at Grosvenor Place and was vigorously courted by Sir Edward Ward's son and heir, Eddie, while attracting the attention of several officers on leave, both British and American, by whom she was wined and dined and taken to the theatre. There were also weekend and longer visits to the country houses of friends. She enjoyed all in all a relentless round of amusement, which must have gone some way to ease the pain of her husband's death in action two years earlier.

In between social engagements Sarah escaped to Leatherhead to be quiet with her children or to entertain close friends at her country house. Principal pastimes there were golf and tennis, either at Pashasham or over at Cherkley Court with her close neighbours, the Beaverbrooks.

May 3rd Lunched at Claridge's with Gail Lucas and two US naval officers, Commander Thompson and Commander Beaslie. I enjoyed the Americans so much. Cmdr Thompson asked me if he might come down to tea with me at Pashasham.

May 5th Commander Thompson came down to tea and stayed on to dinner, returned to London afterwards. I do like him.

May 8th Went up to London this afternoon to stay with Dorothy Barrington-Ward. We dined at home and went to see Maud Allan dance. We all thought her very poor.

Maud Allan, a Canadian dancer, was often compared to Isadora Duncan. She was usually scantily dressed on the stage and caused a sensation in London and elsewhere. Sarah's comment suggests she was shocked rather than merely disappointed by the dancer's performance.

May 9th I got up late and lunched at the Berkeley with Lady Edward Gleichen and Capt. Stoker. Capt. Stoker came shopping with me and we had tea together. Met Bobbie Harris in the street. Great surprise. I haven't seen him since my wedding at Nashville. He was a groomsman. I dined with him tonight and with Commander Thompson. We went to see *Hotch-Potch* which was awful. Am dead tired.

May 12th Lunched today at the Ritz with Bobbie Harris and Commander Thompson. Afterwards went to see Flora Guest. Dined at home quietly and retired early. Big naval feat today. *Vindictive* sunk in Ostend harbour to block submarine base [Zeebrugge].

May 19th Played tennis at the Beaverbrooks, my first game this season. Met a lot of Russian Embassy men but could not feel very agreeable with them, when I think how they have let us down in this war.

May 20th Went to London to lunch at Claridge's with Eddie, on leave from his course at Cambridge. Big air raid on London last night, 200 casualties and six Gothas shot down. After lunch we went to see where the bomb was dropped in King Street.

May 24th Dull, cloudy day. Miss Amos gave notice and was horrid. Said she was not treated as a lady etc. A rank injustice. I've done my utmost to treat her as I would anybody else and I will *not* let it worry me, as it is so false and my conscience is clear. She has proved to me that she doesn't even possess common decency.

May 26th Went to Cherkely Court to spend the night. Max Beaverbrook showed us a wonderful war film called *Hearts of the World* by D.W. Griffiths. Campbell Stuart, Lord Rothermere and others there. Interesting evening.

May 31st News very bad today. Germans have captured Soissons and got to the Marne. Played a few holes of golf on the links with Mrs Mackay.

June 2nd Very hot day. Max and Gladys Beaverbrook came to tea. Played tennis in very scanty attire. Max is a most peculiar man and I can't decide whether I like him or not.

June 3rd Lovely day. New gardener came, a wounded soldier, and was busy with him all morning.

June 5th Took Betty up to London today to stay at Sussex Gardens. Went to opening of U.S. Canteen at Grosvenor Gardens, where I am working with Marie Saunderson. Dined with Flora Guest and met Sir John and Lady Lavery, Sir Lionel Earle, Johnny Dodge [Flora's son, home on leave]. Lady Lavery is very pretty and amusing and does all the talking for the entire party.

June 20th Came up to London today to sell with Lady Herbert at the Flower Show in Trafalgar Square. Lunched at Claridge's with Commander Thompson. It simply poured all afternoon and we consequently didn't make much money with the flowers. Returned home this afternoon. Eddie finished his Staff Course today.

June 21st Came up to London today, lunched with Eddie and afterwards met Sir Edward and Dame Eva Anstruther at Paddington and took the train with them to Blagdon [Somerset], arriving 7.15. Long journey. The place is charming, also the house. We are all very happy here. Longest day of the year. We walked down to the lake after dinner and stayed until 10.30pm.

June 22nd Eddie and Sir Edward went fishing on the lake. Eva and I got up late in time for lunch. Went for walk in the afternoon and went out after dinner in a boat fishing but caught nothing. The wind was too high. Shall never forget the glorious view from the boat, the change of light and the sunset, simply heavenly. I feel so happy here. I never felt there would be such a thing again.

June 23rd Lazy day. Weather fine. Eva and I took a long walk over the downs. The country is ideal, one feels the peace of it all, no aeroplanes flying overhead, no guns practising in the distance.
Eddie and I walked to the boathouse and watched the moon rise. Like the place more and more each day.

June 24th Wet day. Had an early dinner. Sir Edward, Eddie, Eva and I went out in the boat fishing. Eddie caught a 5 lb trout. Great excitement.

June 25th Lovely day. Sir Edward and Eddie fished all morning. In the afternoon we went for a long drive through three lovely villages and all went to the lake after dinner. Wonderful watching the sunset and the shades of night falling fast. Eddie caught another trout today.

June 26th Wonderful sunny day. Eva and I started off at 10.30 in a little farmcart with pony, I driving. We drove to Cheddar and back 20 miles. We had lunch in a funny little inn and bought cheeses and visited Gough's Cave, which we disliked intensely, and half way through refused to go any further, much to the amazement of the Guide. The gatekeeper was most 'inhuman' and returned us our money. We landed back at 5.30, having had a most amusing but trying day. I like being with Dame Eva. She is a delightful companion and so clever.

June 27th I went fishing this morning. No luck. Eddie and I went for a beautiful walk through the fields to the downs. Eva and I were tired and went to bed early. The others went off fishing.

June 28th Wonderful day. Intended to return today but Joan can't come to Pashasham for the weekend, as she has to go somewhere with Princess Mary, so am delighted to stay over.

June 29th Very hot. I caught my first trout, great excitement. I really like fishing, when there are results. Sir Edward has given me a hen and ten little chicks to take home to Pashasham. He is so kind to me.

June 30th Hot again. Got up late. After lunch we managed to get a motor to take us to Weston-super-Mare, where we spent the afternoon by the sea. Very pretty place but much of a muchness. We all feel very sad that the party is breaking up. Have had such a happy time.

July 1st Left Blagdon at 10.30 this morning. Motored to Bristol and caught the train to London. Glad to get home to the children but feel lonely. Bud [her sister-in-law] and Rene dined here tonight.

July 4th All London is celebrating Independence Day. The spirit of unity of the two countries is most impressive. Lunched with Capt. Winn and Eddie and went afterwards to the famous baseball game between Army and Navy. The King presented the ball to the pitcher. All the Royalties were there and 5000 people. Bud and Rene gave a big dinner at the Ritz and we danced afterwards.

July 7th Sunday. Sir Edward, Eva and Louise Edvina came down for the day. Louise wasn't as gracious as she might have been and annoyed me on the subject of my private affairs.

June 8th I was 'cashier' today at the Canteen and felt very nervous. Eddie has to leave for Italy on 11th. It will be sad to see him go but war is war and what have we to say?

July 13th Came this weekend to spend weekend with Mme Vigliano at Ascot. Played tennis at Mrs Stern's, who is an Austrian by birth but has sons in the British Army. I can't forget the fact that she is an enemy alien. Mrs Arthur Vincent, Mrs van der Ault, Major Saunderson and Marie and M. Vigliano were there. Dined and played bridge at the Grange. I find Mme Vigliano most attractive and sympathetic.

July 15th Dull and muggy. Came to London to the Canteen. Do not feel well at all. Had tea with Joan and returned home soon after. Found a letter from Eddie, which cheered me up awfully. Big German offensive began today. Oh, if it will only end this war.

July 20th Went out early on my bike for a little exercise. Over to lunch with Gladys Beaverbrook and stayed on to dinner. That menage is not going well. Faults on both sides. Lord B. came down in the afternoon and we played tennis together after tea. There is a lot I might say but perhaps it is wiser not to.

July 21st Continued showers. A letter from Eddie from Paris came this afternoon. Lord Beaverbrook asked me to go over for dinner, so I did and he motored me home.

July 27th Went early this morning to Victoria Station to go to Eastbourne for a weekend with Mrs Reynolds. But, after standing in a queue for an hour, there were no more tickets to be had until mid-day. The queue extended out into the street, so great were the crowds. I arrived in Eastbourne very late in the afternoon. I think it is a lovely place and I like being with Mrs Reynolds. It is very quiet.

July 29th We motored over to Bexhill today and had lunch there, then went to a Christian Science meeting. Tonight we dined at the Grand Hotel and listened to the band.

The above is the first of three references in these diaries and letters to Christian Science. Although Sarah herself never embraced it as a way of life, a number of her friends did – Mrs Reynolds, Lord Dufferin, Mrs Freddy Guest, and indeed her old friend Flora Guest, and later Lady Grimthorpe. In 1918 a number of people bereaved by the Great War sought comfort in many different beliefs. This was undoubtedly one.

July 30th Returned to London this afternoon. Met Orian and we stayed the night at Sussex Gardens. Odd feeling to be in the house again. We went to the theatre to see *Tails Up* with Cmdr. Thompson and Capt. Foley and went back to the latter's flat for supper. Play very poor but we enjoyed the evening.

July 31st Returned home early this morning, as Nurse goes for her holiday. I am taking her place. Orian is coming to stay with me, until she goes to Boulogne to V.A.D. Feeling miserable today.

Aug. 1st Bright day. This afternoon Mrs Mackay, two wounded officers, one Col. Pope of Ottawa, a friend of Fred's, and others came to tea and tennis.

Aug. 6th Orian and I went up to London and were told at the bank that Bart McLennan was killed on Saturday. My heart is sick for her, as they were in love. She was very much broken up. What does it all mean? Why should she have all this? It is a terrible tragedy. Lunched with Lord and Lady Northcliffe. He doesn't think war will end for years.

Aug. 7th The children are with me at Sussex Gardens. Dined with Campbell Stuart at Claridge's with two other people. Can't remember their names. We went to see Arnold Bennett's play, *The Title*, a skit on the new titles, K.B.E. Most amusing and very clever. Campbell, being one of these new Knights, was very amused.

Aug. 8th Orian came back to Pashasham. She is being very brave but feeling Bart's loss deeply. The Canadians have fought magnificently and are greatly praised.

Aug. 13th Orian received orders to leave Saturday for France. I will miss her terribly but it is the right thing for her just now.

Aug. 16th Went to London with Orian to see her off from Charing Cross station. She looked so nice in her uniform. Afterwards Capt. Foley took me to Paddington and put me on the train. I came down to Lady Holt's house, Cranborne Grange, Windsor Forest, for weekend. I've had a hot discussion with Lady H. and told her some facts, controlled myself rather well, considering all things.

I can only hazard a guess as to why Lady Holt and Sarah had words on this occasion. Lady Holt was from Montreal and a close friend of Fred's family. Sarah had been widowed for over two years and was undoubtedly enjoying a busy social life in London. But to some, especially the older women, she was probably seen as a flighty widow who ought to be leading a quieter life. Doubtless Lady Holt told her so.

Aug. 18th Got up only in time for lunch and was fearfully tired. After lunch we drove over to Mrs Stern's at Ascot for tennis. Met a crowd of people there, most of them members of the Dudley Ward family. Godfrey-Fausset, Major Poullet, Sir Albert Stanley, the man who made the Government have tanks in the Army, Mrs van der Hyte etc.

Aug. 19th Left early for London to Canteen. Came home feeling very tired. Nurse returned from her holiday Saturday.

Aug. 21st Trott left for her holiday today. This afternoon I took the children and Nurse for a drive and we had tea out of our tea basket in a meadow near Cobham. The Allies continue to advance on the Western Front. Fearful Canadian casualties.

Aug. 22nd Lovely day. Betty and I went into the woods to find wood for the fires. Coal is so scarce, we are gathering all the wood possible. I went on my bicycle to Oxshott Common to have tea with the children. One wouldn't see more beautiful heather in Scotland . . . the evenings are so lonely.

Aug. 23rd Went to London in search of a cook. Mme Vigliano and I shopped together after the Canteen. Dined with Capt. Foley and went to see *As You Were*, translation of the Revue, *Plus Ça Change*. Not so good in English. I like Capt. Foley, a nice, interesting, ugly little man.

Aug. 27th Spent the morning with the Coal Controller about my ration, then down by the 2.0 train to stay with Eva Anstruther at Pan's Garden, Beaulieu in the New Forest. After tea Eva and I went over to Lord Montagu's house, which is the show place and centre of Beaulieu. I laughed to myself the way Lady Montagu, knowing I was American, asked me if I would like to do a tour of the place and see 'the historical things'.

Aug. 29th We went over to Southampton today by boat. Made a round of the old shops and bought a few things. Place is crowded with American soldiers and one saw the *Olympic* and many other transport ships that are bringing over thousands of my fellow countrymen to try and finish the war.

Aug. 30th Quiet day. Some people came to lunch, then we went by pony cart, with our tea in a basket, to Buckler's Hard, an old shipping place, where wooden ships were built in olden days. All Metropolitan Police have struck in London, attacked the Special Constables, rather rough times altogether. They haven't been treated fairly.

The Metropolitan Police went on strike in August 1918 to achieve recognition of their trade union. The 'Specials', who moved in to keep order, were seen as strike-breakers and suffered some violence. Sir Edward Ward, who had been a distinguished soldier, became involved in his capacity as Honorary Commandant-in-Chief of the Metropolitan Special Constabulary.

Aug. 31st Sunday. When Lady Ridley left after tea, Eva and I went over to the old Abbey at Beaulieu and the ruins. I stayed on to church alone. This place has a funny effect on me. I feel so strongly a physical presence, it is very wonderful. After Evensong, I waited for the Vicar, who took me over the place again and explained all about it. Very delightful day.

Sept. 1st Eva, her daughter Joyce and I went for a tramp in the New Forest and picked blackberries. Sir Edward arrived this afternoon, after the Police strike was settled and was most interesting on the subject. I had a long, serious talk with him alone.

Sept. 2nd Left early for London and went to Canteen. Met Lilah [Fellowes] after and went to hospital to see her brother, Capt. O'Brien, who has to lie up for three months, poor thing. Went home and found a wonderful lot of letters, including one from Lord Shaughnessy. Having a dreadful time getting a cook. We shall soon have to do our own work.

Sept 4th Went into Leatherhead on my bike to see about a cook. Joan came to stay, looking prettier than ever. After tea Joan and I played a weird game of golf, losing three balls each.

Sept. 9th Met at Canteen James Stokes, a childhood acquaintance, who is in the US Flying Corps. Afterwards had tea with him and heard all the Nashville news.

Sept. 11th I am trying hard to let Sussex Gardens again for the winter. Some people looked over it today and I hope they will take it. Heard tonight that a CPR boat has been sunk with George Weir on board. He was Fred's best friend and our best man. So sad, he was on leave to Canada. The Empress of Russia and her daughters have been brutally murdered.

Sept. 16th Hard day at Canteen. General Biddle had US War Secretary Baker and party to lunch there. He is a most insignificant-looking little man. Dreamt I was dying last night. Awful sensation.

Sept. 17th Very busy about the house all morning. Have had offers to sell my Lease but too late now. I've decided to go back to London this winter. This afternoon I cycled into Leatherhead, where I met Gladys Beaverbrook and we went on to Cherkley to play tennis. We had very good sets but I do not enjoy the other part, there is so little really in common. One feels an atmosphere so strongly.

Sept. 24th Am stopping at Sussex Gardens for a week. Went with Capt. Foley to see Gertrude Elliot in *Eyes of Youth*, very enjoyable play. There is a very serious railway strike. No trains running for two days, all soldiers and wounded held up. I believe

German agents must be at the back of these strikes, which are such a menace to England.

Sept. 25th Had my hair washed in afternoon. Went to First Night of *Hello, America*. Parts of the revue were poor but Elsie Janis is charming and excellent. We are all rationed with coal, light and gas. It will be very cold this winter, as the allowance is small.

Towards the end of September 1918 the war news began to improve and a new mood of optimism swept the country. But Sarah's mood remained much the same, her moments of elation and enjoyment of a busy social life giving way to bouts of deep depression and loneliness, causing her frequently to feel unwell. Although she was surrounded by wonderful friends and male admirers in profusion, the pain of her husband's death and her anxiety for the future still kept her spirits low. It is probable that, deep down, she was attempting to take refuge in a crowded life, both in London and at Pashasham Lodge, from the gnawing doubt as to whether she had done the right thing in removing herself and her children three thousand miles away from Montreal and the Shaughnessys, who were, after all, her dead husband's family.

Sept. 27th Dined with Capt. Foley at the Ritz. Feeling seedy, so went to bed early.

Sept. 28th Returned home this morning. Railway strike is over. Was a most disgraceful thing.

Oct. 1st War news is most encouraging. Bulgarians are suing for peace. Steady advance of Allies on all fronts. Have a terrible cold, feel so ill. Went to bed after lunch.

Oct. 2nd Still in bed, feeling miserable. I must have 'flu. One feels depressed. Bulgaria surrendered today. General unconditional armistice. Allied success on all fronts. At last tide has turned and we seem to be moving towards victory.

Oct. 4th Am a little better today. Sat on balcony outside

bedroom in the sun this morning. Had to spank Tommy tonight, so disobedient. The effect was wonderful. Have sold my chickens for £28, a very successful season.

Oct. 6th German Chancellor, Prince Max of Baden, cries peace. Wishes for an armistice to talk peace. Things are moving fast but hope we won't stop until we have made the Germans suffer to the last degree for all their crimes and for all the lives sacrificed. The thought of the war being over brings back the terrible reality of all one has lost. Quiet Sunday alone at home with the children.

Oct. 7th German note sent to President Wilson asking for an armistice. Enemy retreating on all fronts. Went to London to Canteen. Had tea with Eva Anstruther. Dined tonight at Claridge's with Cmdr. Thompson and Leigh Noyes, whom I hadn't seen for ten years.
Nice evening.

Oct. 8th Am staying at Sussex Gardens. Horrible rainy weather. Marie Saunderson and I lunched at the Ritz. Huge crowds there, most cheerful and gay, more pre-war than otherwise. Prince of Wales lunching there too. They are becoming very democratic. Dined with Capt. Foley at the Berkeley. Cambrai has been captured.

Oct. 9th Raining again. Got up late. Had letters from my brother, Thomas, and Eddie Ward. Had tea with Joan, where I met her mother [Lady Strafford] and Lady Mary Trefusis, Lady-in-Waiting to the Queen. Very stiff and dull, I thought. Dined tonight at the Ritz with Cmdr. Noyes and went to *The Maid of the Mountains*, enjoyed it very much.

Oct. 10th Returned home today. President Wilson's answer to German Note is 'unconditional surrender'. Heard Lord Shaughnessy has resigned from the Canadian Pacific. Wonder what it all means.

Oct. 12th Sent off important letter to Lord Shaughnessy about money and the children's future. Eva and Sir Edward came for weekend. Headquarters rang up Sir Edward at 11.0 at night saying word had come through that Germans had accepted all Wilson's fourteen points. Great excitement, as it must mean peace very soon.

Oct. 13th Awoke early and got all the papers published for further news. But find we aren't as near peace as we thought. Many problems yet to be solved.

Oct. 17th In London. Wilson and Germany continue to exchange Notes. Lunched with Lady Holt. Dined with Cmdr. Thompson and went afterwards to a party at Mrs Grant's. A gathering of the so-called *haute monde*. First real function I've attended since March. We had music and danced. Lady Diana Manners and all that set were there. I was much amused and interested. Oscar Guest, looking as dirty as ever. Liked Capt. Bulkeley-Johnson. Got home at 1 o'clock. Lille was captured today.

Oct. 21st To London to canteen. Terrible fog. Tonight went to General Biddle's house to a dance. Enjoyed it very much. Seemed a bit like old times – everybody was there. Very gay. But I'm afraid I can never enjoy things as I used to.

Oct. 22nd Heard that Eddie is ill in hospital with bronchitis but not serious. Very busy at house. Dined tonight with Clara Scott.

Oct. 24th Quiet day. Busy packing to move back to Sussex Gardens on 28th. Will be happy to be in my own house again with my own things. There is a terrible epidemic of influenza all over the world. Thousands of deaths reported in England last week. It looks like the end of all things.

Oct. 29th Lunched with Joan. Met there Admiral and Mrs Victor Stanley, Admiral Mark Kerr and Major Reginald Seymour. Adml. Stanley charming. Liked him the best. The Duke of Connaught telephoned this morning and asked himself to tea. He stayed an hour and was as nice as ever.

7 Sarah (left) in Hyde Park with the Marquess of Dufferin and Ava, Lady Joan Mulholland and Lord Claud Hamilton, 1919.

8 Sarah by Bertram Park, 1919.

CRIMEAN COLLAPSE : BRITISH FLEET'S TASK

The Daily Mirror

CERTIFIED CIRCULATION LARGER THAN THAT OF ANY OTHER DAILY PICTURE PAPER

No. 5,320. | Registered at the G.P.O. as a Newspaper. | TUESDAY, NOVEMBER 16, 1920 | [20 PAGES] | One Penny.

THE PRINCE OF WALES AT A WEST END WEDDING

The crowd outside St. Peter's waiting for arrival of the bride and bridegroom and their friends.—(D. M.)

Captain Legh and his bride leaving the church after the ceremony.—(Daily Mirror.)

The Prince of Wales was the principal wedding guest. The Prince leaving after conclusion of the service.

Captain the Hon. Piers Legh, son of Lord and Lady Newton, married yesterday to the Hon. Mrs. Alfred Shaughnessy at St. Peter's, Eaton-square, London, the vicar, the Rev. Austin Thompson, officiating. The Prince of Wales honoured the bride and bride-groom by his presence, and a large number of other distinguished friends were also present. There was no reception. The Duke of Connaught was among those who sent presents. The honeymoon is to be spent at the bridegroom's old home, Lyme Park.

9 Front-page spread of Sarah's wedding to Joey, November 1920.

10

11

10 Snapshot of the Duke of Connaught
   taken by Sarah at Bagshot Park, 1922.
11 Pastel drawing of Sarah by Olive Snell
   (Mrs Ebenezer Pike), 1923.

Oct. 31st Lunched with Lady Ross, then she, Flora and I visited American hospital in Tottenham. The men were delighted to see us. One felt that one had made them happy by going. Turkey surrendered today. Now out of the war. Austria will probably be next. Not feeling very well, so retired to bed early.

Nov. 3rd Flora came to lunch and we went to see Hartland Patterson, who is badly wounded, in hospital. Very tired, went to bed early. My cook has 'flu! Having a bad time trying to get servants. Austria is out of the war.

Nov. 7th Took children to tea at Flora's with Mrs. Gilliatt's [sic] children. (Lily Gilliat, formerly wife of the eccentric Marquess of Anglesey, was now married to Jack Gilliat.) Got a rumour of peace, which was discredited. Dined there and went to Grafton Galleries to dance.

Nov. 10th Joan and I walked in park in the morning. I lunched with Dorothy Barrington-Ward and went out with children in the afternoon. Dined with Major Harding and Joan at Ritz. Kaiser abdicated today.

Nov. 11th WAR IS OVER. Armistice signed by Germans at 5 o'clock this morning. Terrific rejoicing. People went mad. Clara, Mary and I went in a taxi to see demonstration in front of Buckingham Palace. Thousands of people had collected there.

King, Queen, Princess Mary and Duke of Connaught came out on the balcony. Eva and I went down to the Lords to hear Armistice Terms read out. My heart is both sad and glad. The memory of dear Fred, who gave his life for victory, which has come at last.

5

Peace out of Pain

Much has been written about the cruel irony that caused many thousands of people who had lost loved ones in the Great War to find themselves engulfed in cheering crowds on Armistice Night. It must have been heart-breaking for some to witness the joy and relief of others whom the long war had left untouched. And yet it was everybody's joy. The whole nation rejoiced. And Sarah was no exception.

Nov. 12th Joan and I lunched at Ritz with Maitland Kersey. Tremendous celebrations still going on. Mrs Goudy, Joan and I went to a very poor concert at Lady Salisbury's in the evening. Dined at Joan's with Cmdr. Thompson and another American and went to the Alhambra. The crowds are mad, we could hardly get through Piccadilly Circus, people jumping on to our taxi etc.

Nov. 16th Joan, the children, her little nephew, Robin Byng, and I took a drive in the afternoon to see the peace celebrations. Later Joan took us all into Buckingham Palace to see the King, Queen and Prince of Wales come in. Dined tonight with Lord and Lady Decies. She is very attractive, he is nice but a bit old and dull.

Nov. 18th Canteen today. Joan, Claud Hamilton, Campbell Stuart and the Barrington-Wards dined with me. Claud told me all about the Prince and the V.A.D.s, which, if known, would cause some trouble. I feel tired and bored. What is the matter with me, I wonder. Old age, perhaps. I pretend to love everything but nobody knows the real truth.

Nov. 22nd Lunched at home with Betty. No place like home and one's own. Met two horribly masculine women today. Motor convoy drivers, hair short etc. Made me all creepy.

Nov. 23rd Arrived down here at Panshanger, Lord Queenborough's house, for weekend. People staying are Lord and Lady Dufferin, Joan, Sir George Clark, Capt Charles Winn and Miss Olive Paget,* Queenborough's daughter. A wonderful house with simply priceless pictures. Have developed a cold and sore throat and feel rather miserable. Danced all evening.

Nov. 24th Rainy day. Do not feel well. I like Lord Dufferin. He is a dear, the best of the party. We sat talking by the fire all afternoon. Feeling so ill, had to retire to bed after tea. Simply hated to do this but could not help it.

Nov. 25th Returned to London. Awful journey. Went straight to bed and called in Dr. Laing, who says I have acute laryngitis. So painful and can get no relief. Was asked to lunch with Connaughts at Clarence House but could not go.

Nov. 26th Not feeling so well. Had to put off General Sykes, Major Harding etc who were lunching with me today. Marie Saunderson came to see me but I could not talk, as my voice left me suddenly.

Nov. 27th Still have no voice. Lord Dufferin sent me some lovely flowers. Flora, Joan and lots of people called today.

Nov. 28th Feeling better. Voice stronger. Lord Queenborough sent some lovely roses roday. Have just received a cruel letter from Lord Shaughnessy, which has hurt me deeply. What a life! Rene came to see me after dinner and we had a heart-to-heart talk. He is a dear and very understanding.

*

---

*She married first Charles Winn, then Sir Adrian Baillie. She lived with the latter at Leeds Castle, Maidstone, Kent.

This is the first hint of Sarah's developing rift with the wealthy, influential Shaughnessy family in Montreal since her original decision to bring her children over to England in 1917. It is clear that reports were reaching Lady Shaughnessy's ears from Canadian friends in London that her widowed daughter-in-law was having a good time, frequently being seen lunching, dining and at the theatre in London with her many gentlemen admirers. In addition, there had been friction earlier on over the matter of the children's religion. Sarah had insisted on her right to bring up her daughter Betty in the Anglican faith, although the two boys were compelled to be baptized as Catholics. The question of the boys' education was looming and Lord Shaughnessy is known to have wanted them sent to Catholic schools in England. Sarah later conceded, when they were quite small, that they should have Catholic instruction from nuns at the Tyburn Convent in Bayswater Road, but with the support later on of her second husband, Piers Legh, the boys both finally attended Church of England schools – Summer Fields, Oxford, and Eton.

That, together with Sarah's enviable social success in London society, was most probably the root cause of this total alienation from Lady Shaughnessy and the less hostile disapproval of her father-in-law, who like all the men in Sarah's life, found her distinctly attractive.

Nov. 29th Feeling much better. Lunched at Clarence House with Connaughts. Met there Lady Randolph Churchill, Lady Georgina Buchanan and her husband and several more people, whose names I forget.

Mr. Doubleday came to dine. Had an awful scene. Shan't forget this evening. He wanted me to marry him.

Nov. 30th Clara Scott came to lunch; Mrs Reynolds to tea; and Lord Dufferin came in at six o'clock. I had a bad fit of coughing while he was here. He had to go, as I was too exhausted to talk. Dined tonight at the Ritz with Col. Mostyn-Owen. I like him so much. Have seen too many people today and am fearfully tired.

Dec. 1st Lunched with Bud and Rene at Claridge's. Marshal Foch and Clemenceau arrived in London today. Great cheers and welcome for them. Foch came to Claridge's, so we saw him. Went to church with Col. Mostyn-Owen. Marie and Mrs Strutt came to tea and we played bridge. Col. Mostyn-Owen stayed to dinner. I feel terribly about him, as I didn't realize he really loved me and wanted to marry me. What am I to do about it all? Am feeling very upset these days.

Dec. 2nd Went to my Canteen today. Have been dazed and have thought of one thing only all day [Lord Dufferin?]. I am as one walking in a dream. Eva came to tea this afternoon.

Dec. 4th Joan lunched here today. Eddie arrived home on leave from Italy and came to tea. I was not as glad to see him as I thought I would be. What is the matter with me? We dined together and went to a play.

Dec. 5th Feel too indifferent to write. A change is coming over me.

Dec. 6th Eva, Eddie and I went to Torquay today for the weekend. Very tiresome journey, arriving after dinner. Was asked to dine to meet Prince Axel of Denmark.

Dec. 7th Torquay is lovely, warm and balmy. I told Eddie today that I had changed and nothing was the same. It is terrible for him and he is desperate. It can't be helped. I feel I can never love him enough to marry him.

Dec. 8th Wonderful warm day. We took walks and drove in the afternoon. I feel too wretched and can hardly wait to get back to London. Everything and everybody is getting on my nerves.

Dec. 9th Returned to London today, very tired. Had dinner on a tray and Joan came in after to see me.

Dec. 10th Had people to lunch. Dined with Eddie and went to the theatre. Had a final break with him and said goodbye.

Dec. 11th Too miserable to write.

Dec. 12th Eddie swears he can't stay away and begs to be friends. Went to the Doubledays' dance at Sunderland House. Met Sir Harry Mainwaring, whom I like very much.

Dec. 13th Lord Shaughnessy came to tea today. Very difficult interview but I put my pride in my pocket and remain on friendly terms for the sake of the children. Dined with Major Pease at the Criterion. Was not in the mood and was bored.

Dec. 15th Filthy day. Lunched with Dorothy B-W. Sir Harry Mainwaring came to tea. Dined at Ritz with Sir George and Lady Perley. Met there Lord Frederick Hamilton. Most amusing person.

Dec. 18th Joan and I went shopping. Dined tonight with Lord Dufferin, General Townshend and Mrs. Darrell. Went to theatre and on to a dance at General Biddle's. Duke of Connaught was there, he came over and talked to me for half an hour. Very amusing to see how the people stared.

Dec. 19th Betty and I went shopping. Lunched alone here. Lord Dufferin came in after tea. Lord Shaughnessy, Bud and Rene dined with me.

Dec. 20th Lunched with Joan and went shopping afterwards. Dined tonight with General Townshend and went on to see *Maid of the Mountains*. Met at dinner Lady Peek, Mrs Fitzgerald, Lord Dufferin. Very amusing evening. General Townshend is too crazy about women to suit me. His own fault.

Dec. 22nd Joan and Lord Dufferin lunched here. Rainy afternoon, so didn't go out. Sir Harry Mainwaring came to tea. Eddie came to dine. Life is very different with him now. He is getting on my nerves.

Dec. 23rd Lunched with Lady Dufferin in their tiny house. Met there Capt. Somerset. Shopped afterwards. Dined with Eddie and went to see *Soldier Boy*. Very poor play.

Dec. 25th Mrs Reynolds lunched quietly with me and we had a nice, long talk. Had Christmas Tree for the children at four. Clara brought hers. Bud, Rene, Lord Shaughnessy, Marguerite [Fred's unmarried sister over with her father from Montreal] Sylvia [Lady Edward] Gleichen, all came. They had a very happy day. Only Joan's little girl [Daphne Mulholland] was ill and couldn't come. Dined tonight at the Carlton with Lord S, family party, rather depressing and I was glad to get home.

Dec. 26th Lunched with Flora, Lionel and Eddie and went to White's Club to see President and Mrs Wilson arrive. Streets were lined by Grenadier soldiers and the reception he received was wonderful. Was tremendously impressed by Mr. Wilson.

Dec. 27th Was invited to meet Mrs. Wilson at American Embassy. Went with Flora. I found Mrs. W charming and delightful with a true Southern manner. Felt quite honoured being asked to meet her. Dined with Freddy Dufferin and went to see *Officers' Mess*. Very poor play but enjoyed the evening.

Dec. 28th Lunched alone today. Went afterwards for a pre-war motor drive through Richmond with Dorothy and Lance B-W.
Sir Harry Mainwaring came to tea. Eddie came to dine. I told him quite definitely that I could never marry him. I do feel so sorry for him, it's terribly hard. However, it's the truth.

Dec. 29th Barrington-Wards and 'Dad' [Lord S.] came to lunch. Went for walk in the afternoon with Freddy [Dufferin]. Major White came to tea and made us scream with laughter. Went later to see Joan. Dined at the Ritz with General and Lady Townshend. Met there Mrs Falk, Col. Repington and Freddy. Lady Townshend's conversation isn't fit for the drawing-room. I was disgusted and shocked.

Sarah does not record in her Diary the arrival by hand on that day, 29 December, of a letter dated 28 December. The text is as follows:

My Darling Sarah,

I have an opportunity of leaving this note and, as long as I have been standing in the dismal City waiting for the President and Mrs Wilson to eat their lunch at the Mansion House, I have had you with me – only in the spirit, of course – but I saw your dear face all the time. I do so love you, darling, you can't imagine how much and I feel so tremendously happy, just bubbling over with it. I wonder if you could manage it to see you for a little tomorrow afternoon. I am sure you can squeeze a small visit in. Do anyhow try and I will ring you up round one and hope you will be a dear and manage something.

Goodnight, Sarah darling, don't be angry with me for writing to you just frankly, I can't help it.

Your loving, Freddy

Dec. 30th Went to canteen, then on to see Joan. Dined tonight with Maitland [Kersey] and took Mr. Doubleday with me. Bud, Rene, 'Dad' and General Lowther there. Was rather bored. Too many family parties.

Dec. 31st Lunched with Mrs Reynolds. Freddy and I went to a cinema afterwards. Had tea with Lady Allan. Dined tonight with Freddy and Lady Dufferin at Ritz. Also there were Joan, Major Harding and Capt. Sage, USA.

Saw the new year in there, then Freddy and I went on afterwards to the Orr-Lewis dance, where we stayed only a short time. Most interesting. May the New Year bring joy and the real things of life.

And so ended 1918, an extraordinary year for Sarah. The Great War that had taken her beloved Fred was now over and she found herself one of many thousands of war widows in London society, many of them with young children, attempting to rebuild their lives and hoping for a happier future. There is no doubt that Sarah's closest friend at this time was Lady Joan Mulholland (née Byng), a daughter of the Earl of Strafford, whose husband, Captain the Hon. Andrew Mulholland, had also been killed in action in France. She was Lady-in-Waiting to Princess Mary until, in 1922, two years after Sarah remarried, she married General [later Field-Marshal] the Earl of Cavan, who had commanded the Guards Division in France and the British troops on the Italian Front. It was plainly Joan who introduced Sarah to her own circle in London, while Sarah, for her part, brought into Joan's life a number of her Canadian friends, such as Lady Holt, Lady Allan, Sir Campbell Stuart, Lord Beaverbrook, Maitland Kersey and others, not to mention various young American and Canadian officers who were over in Europe for the war. Thus the two young widows had a high old time, considering all things.

Of all the men who appear to have been either infatuated or actually in love with Sarah her most persistent admirer was Eddie Ward. However, as 1918 gave way to 1919, a new beau appears in her life in the shape of Freddy, the Marquess of Dufferin and Ava, whose wife Brenda was most likely aware of her husband's feelings but, evidently bearing no malice, continued to be friendly.

6

On with the Dance

As the year 1919 dawned, Sarah must have wondered what, if any, new and exciting direction her life might take over the ensuing months. On 28 October of the previous year, shortly before the Armistice, she had given up Pashasham Lodge and moved back for good with the children and their nurse to 51 Sussex Gardens. From now on London was to be her permanent home, with all it had to offer. As to her love life at this time, it seems that Eddie Ward was moving out and Lord Dufferin was moving in. But a potential stepfather for her three Canadian children was not yet to be seen on the horizon.

Jan. 20th [*1919*] Returned home this afternoon from a weekend at Craigweil House, Bognor, with Sir Arthur du Cros. Lovely day. We played tennis and bridge after dinner. Tonight I dined at Ritz with Freddy Dufferin.

Jan. 23rd Betty's 6th birthday. Lord Shaughnessy, Mr. and Mrs Arthur Crichton and Lord and Lady Dufferin came to lunch. Daphne Mulholland and Jean Crichton came to tea with the children in the nursery.

Jan. 28th Went to my Canteen. Lunched with Mrs Leggatt. Met there Doubledays, Gen. Townshend, Lord Sandwich and the Duke of Rutland. Went to Lady Mainwaring's dance in the evening.

Jan. 30th Dined Lord Fitzwilliam, went to a play and on to Lord Furness' big ball. Eddie Ward and Mrs Pike [Olive Snell, the artist] were in the party. A lady lost her petticoat at the ball, which nobody will ever forget.

Jan. 31st Went with Mrs Tombo to Old Vic to see French plays.

Feb. 2nd Lord S. and Redmonds to lunch. Dined with Maitland Kersey and Lilah Fellowes. Awfully bored. All waiters in London have gone on strike. No restaurants open.

Feb. 8th Came to stay at Hinchingbrooke for weekend with Lord and Lady Sandwich. House party are Mrs Leggatt, Mrs Burton, Gen. Sir Charles Townshend, Lieut McCaulay, R.N. and a Mr. Horner from New York. Terrible bore! Most lovely place, wonderful pictures.

Feb. 9th Sunday, got up late, walked round place. Snow on the ground. Lady Sandwich is ill but Mrs Leggatt acted as hostess. The General is too awful with his stories of wine, women and song. Curious how many men's brains are so developed on those lines.

Feb. 15th Lunched with Mrs Pike and met there Col. Pike and Mrs Maxmuller. I like them all very much. Olive Pike's drawings are really wonderful. Dined in with Freddy.

Feb. 18th Lunched with 'Dad' at Carlton. Dined tonight in Mrs Paget's party to see *Scandal*. At last moment both Pagets got 'flu and we all went on without them – total strangers. Most awkward. Others were Mrs Chapman and Capt. and Mrs Fletcher. Perfectly awful evening.

Feb. 21st Lunched Joan, met there Lord Queenborough, Mrs Gardner and Freddy. Joan and I took Betty and Daphne in afternoon to Royal Stables at Buckingham Palace to see the State coaches and were shown round by Sir Charles Fitzwilliam, the Crown Equerry. Children loved it all. Clemenceau was shot by an anarchist but not badly hurt. The world is going Bolshevist mad.

Feb. 23rd Sunday. Lord S. and I motored out to Richmond Park to lunch with Georgina, Lady Dudley. General Bobby White was there [he took part in the famous Jameson Raid in South Africa].

The house was given to Lady Dudley by King Edward, who was a great friend of hers.

Feb. 25th Lunched with Eddie. I find it most difficult to keep the peace. However, what else can I expect?

Joan and the Gleichens dined and we went to an evening party at St James's Palace, given by the King and Queen for Princess Patricia [the Duke of Connaught's daughter]. A very pre-war, elaborate affair, we had great fun. All her presents were on view and they are magnificent. She seems very happy.

Feb. 27th Lord Shaughnessy and I went to Princess Patricia's wedding at Westminster Abbey. It was a lovely ceremony and the bride looked beautiful. The crowds in the streets were tremendous, a sight one will never forget. I lunched with Lord and Lady Decies and met there Mr. Fisher of New Zealand. Dined with Lord Queenborough, Max Beaverbrook there.

Feb. 28th Lunched alone at home and went in afternoon to see Freddy, who is in a Nursing Home. Eddie dined here, rather sad parting, as he sails for America tomorrow. I feel such a brute.

March 2nd Lunched with Joan. Brenda Dufferin was there, Capt. Butler and Capt. Legh. After lunch Joan and I went to sign the books at Clarence House and Buckingham Palace. Dined in quietly.

Sarah Shaughnessy was not to know that her lunch engagement that day, 2 March 1919, seemingly a day like any other day, was to prove a turning-point in her life. On 5 March she celebrated her twenty-eighth birthday.

March 5th Awful rainy day. Dined with Joan in a party and went to see *Buzz-Buzz*, the best revue on at present. A very enjoyable evening.

March 9th Sunday. Went to tea with Mr. Davis in his flat. The Pagets were there and Capt. Legh and we danced. Dined at home and went afterwards to a small dance at Mrs. Orr-Lewis' house. It was quite fun, until we had to walk all the way home from Grosvenor Square, there being no taxis to be had.

March 14th Lunched at Ritz with Lady Peek. Dined at Criterion with Capt. Legh. Mrs Paget and Mr. Davis were in the party. It was great fun dancing.

March 15th Went down to Leatherhead to see caretaker at Pashasham Lodge. Had lunch at the Mackays. Came back to London. Lord Claud Hamilton came to tea. Dined with Mrs. Pike but was three quarters of an hour late, as could not get a taxi. Lord Churchill was there and we went on to Lady Peek's dance. Lord Claud came too and brought me home.

March 17th Dined with Mrs Richard Bethell. Others there were Lord Wodehouse and Don Pedro de Zulueta. Went on afterwards to Capt. Cator's dance. Had a wonderful evening.

March 18th Lord Wodehouse came to tea, also Mrs Paget. Lord W. is attractive but I don't know yet whether I like him or not. [Years later Sarah's daughter by her second marriage, Diana, married Lord Wodehouse's son, by then Earl of Kimberley, but the marriage did not last.]

March 20th Lunched with Lord Wodehouse at the Ritz and went afterwards with Lady Peek to call on Mrs Davis, the American Ambassador's wife, who didn't impress me very much.

March 21st Lunched with Mrs Cazalet. Went with Olive Pike to my singing lesson. Joan, Lord Claud and Capt. Legh dined here and we went on to the Grafton Galleries and danced.

March 25th Lunched with Major Brind and went afterwards to see the Russian Ballet. Was bored to tears, as I dislike this man. He is a nuisance. Went to tea in the House of Lords with Lord Churchill. The Duke of Marlborough joined us and I listened to the speeches until seven. Dined with Lord Queenborough and went to opera to hear *Manon Lescaut.*

March 26th Joan, Gail, Lord Claud, Oscar Guest and Rene Escudier came to lunch. Latter I haven't seen in eight years. [He was her beau in Paris at whose house she met Puccini.] Had my first singing lesson today with Gerald Allen. He likes my voice but says I am run down and have lost my vitality with war strain. Perfectly true too. Capt. Legh came to tea. We had such a nice talk.

March 28th Capt. Legh asked me to lunch but, as Joan was coming to me, I asked him too, so we three lunched at home. Lord Wodehouse dined with me and we went on to Mrs Bethell's dance, which was great fun. Loved the evening.

April 2nd Lunched at Ritz with Capt. Legh. The Prince of Wales was to have come but something prevented him at the last moment. Dined at Claridge's with Lord Churchill and came to bed early.

April 6th Victor Churchill motored me down to Leatherhead to collect some belongings.

April 7th Victor Churchill, Freddy Dufferin and Baron de Stoeckl came to lunch with me. Dined with Dufferins and Lord Dalmeny at Claridge's and went on to a dance at Martin's.

April 8th Lunch with Lady Allan and to my surprise Flora Guest was there, first time I'd seen her since we fell out, most embarrassing. Dined tonight with Lord Claud Hamilton and met at dinner Lady Coke, Joan, Mrs Leigh, Lord and Lady Cromer, Capt. Bulkeley-Johnson, Capt. Aly Harding, and General Trotter. We went on to Capt. Legh's dance. Met the Prince of Wales for the first time and danced with him most of the evening. Had a wonderful time. Prince and Princess Arthur of Connaught, Prince Albert [later George VI], Princess Mary, and Lady Patricia Ramsay were there.

April 9th Mrs Bethell, Capt. George Graves and Don Pedro de Zulueta came to dine and we went on to the Chaplins' dance. Sat most of the evening with Capt. Legh. Was so tired. This life is too much for me.

April 11th Lunched with Freddy Dufferin. Poor dear, he is so worried and sad. Wish I could help him but am afraid I can't. Victor Churchill and I went to Gen. Biddle's dance, which was great fun. The Prince of Wales and Prince Albert were there and many others. Have changed my mind about Lord Wodehouse.

The sadness and worry of Lord Dufferin was presumably caused by his infatuation with Sarah and the fact that he was not free to marry her, even if he had wanted to. Brenda Dufferin was a good, loyal wife who had borne him two children and he was a religious man, as well as being vulnerable to any scandal – for he occupied an important position in public life. He had an excellent war record and had won several decorations, and later he was to become Speaker of the Senate of Northern Ireland and Vice-Administrator of the Province of Ulster.

April 13th Sunday. Went to church with Freddy and walked afterwards in the park with him, Joan and Claud. Freddy came back to lunch with me. Dined tonight with Joan. Claud and Capt. Legh were there. Very nice evening.

April 15th Went for a walk with Capt. Legh. I like him so much. Orian came to lunch. She is in wonderful spirits and so plucky. Dined with Capt. Legh at the Criterion, enjoyed it very much. Shan't forget today.

April 17th Had a three hours' interview with Flora Guest, who succeeded in making me thoroughly miserable. She has unjustly accused me and my conscience is quite clear and right will out in time, I know. She is a dangerous woman and I am greatly disappointed in her. I believed in her but now . . . dined with Victor.

Sarah had known Flora Guest in Montreal since before her marriage to Fred. Flora, an older woman and a powerful, generous personality, had taken Sarah under her wing when she came to live in London in 1917, introducing her to all sorts of interesting people. No reason is given why the two women fell out but it may be assumed that Sarah's involvement at this time with so many different men, married and unmarried, was causing talk in certain circles and not a little jealousy.

April 19th Lunched with Freddy and went to see a matinee of *Abraham Lincoln*. Wonderful acting but, being a Southerner, I could not entirely agree with the play. It was very inaccurate. Dined with Freddy at Claridges's. London is deserted. Everyone away.

April 20th Gail and Freddy came to lunch. I sat in the park this morning. Cold again. Wore my fur coat. Victor took me and Betty out in his motor this afternoon. We drove down to Wrotham to see Joan. Victor dined in with me. He is an odd person. Awfully nice and so frank. [Apart from being a page to Queen Victoria, Viscount Churchill was Lord Chamberlain to King Edward VII. He became Chairman of the Great Western Railway Company.]

Towards the end of the month Sarah's exhausting social life was interrupted by a grim journey across the Channel to France, undertaken voluntarily in the company of her friend Joan Mulholland. Both widows were in search of their respective husbands' graves. The Diary speaks for itself:

April 28th The most terrible day I've ever seen, bitterly cold rain and terrific wind. Joan and I left early this morning for Boulogne. We hesitated crossing when we got to Folkestone but decided to go on. Channel was very rough. Maitland Kersey and Capt. Launcelot Lowther travelled with us and we lunched with them at Boulogne. Joan and I are staying at the Hotel du Nord, which is a rest home for Red Cross nurses. As we are wearing V.A.D. uniform, we were allowed in. Walked around Boulogne in the afternoon and arranged for tomorrow's trip.

The V.A.D's are making a great fuss over us and are most kind. We went to bed early.

April 29th Capt. Murphy, Head of the Canadian Red Cross, called for us in his motor at eight o'clock and took us up to the British Front to see our husbands' graves. We passed through St. Omer, at one time GHQ, Cassel, Poperinghe and through Ypres to Zillerbeke. Joan found her husband's grave in a cemetery just outside Ypres. Also her uncle's. Then we went on to the big Canadian cemetery called Maple Copse to try and find Fred's grave but in vain. We walked five miles over the country but with no luck. The whole place is a mass of shell holes, barbed wire, bones, dud shells and horrible smells and we saw the carcass of a dead horse. Capt. Murphy told us there were still German corpses buried in the dug-outs. The wind and rain were so terrible, I could go on no longer. I began to feel ill, so turned away disappointed at not finding my dear one's place of rest. I would have gone on, had I felt strong enough to walk in the gale, which nearly blew one away. I don't regret one bit having come, even though I didn't find the grave, for it was to me just like walking on Holy ground and being brought so close to the Heaven which holds our loved ones. It gave me a new and better understanding of what our brave men endured. I have not given up hope and shall try again to find the spot.

We had lunch at Poperinghe, where this famous girl, 'Ginger' used to serve the soldiers.

We returned to the hotel at seven and went to bed straight after dinner. I have never been so tired in all my life. This has been a wonderful experience, seeing the battlefields of Flanders. Masses of German prisoners were 'clearing up' the barbed wire, filling in trenches, collecting shells and moving the graves. How one loathes the very sight of these people. We saw some Star Shells being fired.

After their distressing visit to the battlefields, Joan Mulholland and Sarah proceeded to Paris for a few days where, from their base at the Ritz, their social life apparently continued unabated.

April 30th We arrived in Paris at 4.30 and were met by my old friend from early days, Rene Escudier, who had reserved rooms for us at the Ritz.

After tea we rested, then dined quietly and retired early, dog tired from yesterday. Today is my wedding anniversary. Seven years today, I married Fred in Nashville. It seems like another world.

May 1st Labor Day. By order of the leaders of the Labor Organization all work was suspended in Paris for 24 hours, to prove their power. No motors, restaurants closed, and soldiers lining the streets but nothing serious happened. Joan and I lunched with Ralph Lambton and spent most of the day at his flat in the rue Henri Moisson. Louise Edvina, Mrs. Long and Major Higgins were there and, for dinner, Comte de Grigne, Mr. Grenfell and Sir Godfrey Thomas.

May 2nd Joan and I went out shopping and to attend to our passports. We went to Les Galeries Lafayettes and Ducerf Scavini. Clothes are *so* expensive, we have brought nothing but thin stockings. Dined tonight with Rene Escudier. Others at dinner were Bettine Grant, Lord Pembroke and the Comte de Perigny. Afterwards we went to a dance at the Perigny's house, given for me by Rene and de Perigny. It was fun but I must say I prefer Englishmen and Americans.

May 3rd We lunched at Ritz with Rene and Mme Escudier, others there were Ralph Lambton and M. Pierre Lafitte. It rained all afternoon, so Joan and I spent the time looking at dresses but not buying anything, as there was nothing for less than a thousand francs. Dined with Ralph Lambton and met Mrs Arthur James, Mrs. Long, Bettine Grant, Melle de Bertecourt, Lady Ridley, Lord Pembroke, Comte de Gangeron, an artist, Lord Cochran and Sir Godfrey Thomas. Went on to Comtesse de Berthier's dance. Great fun. Received a love letter from M. Lafitte, whom I met for the first time today. He left a note for me at the Ritz, Frenchmen are funny. Hard to read but it said:

Chère Madame,
    Vous allez dire: 'Les français sont tous les mêmes!' Eh, bien, oui, nous sommes tous épris de beauté and de charme. C'est pourquoi je suis un peu triste a l'idée que vous allez partir et que je ne vous reverrai peut-être jamais plus! J'ai eu pour

vous une sympathie mondaine et irresistible. Il y a dans votre visage tant de gravité et tant de douceur souriante que, pour la première fois de ma vie, me voilà troublé par une femme qui n'est pas une française! Je passerai à Ritz ce soir vers 10 heures mais comme je ne serai pas habillé, je voudrais vous voir ailleurs que dans la salle. Si vous n'y êtes pas, je tâcherai de vous téléphoner demain. Excusez moi et croyez à toute ma sympathie, Pierre Lafitte.

Sarah must have somehow encouraged M. Lafitte, for he wrote to her again at Sussex Gardens in London, once more declaring:

> Je pense souvent à vous et à votre visage tour à tour si grave et si souriant. Mais il va falloir que je chasse ce souvenir car il tournerai a l'idée fixe . . . et je serais capable de devenir amoureux de vous. Voyez-vous ce catastrophe . . . à mon âge! J'éspère que vous vous décidez à revenir à Paris. Venez danser un fox-trot avec moi!
>
> Avec mes sentiments les plus sincères,
> Pierre Lafitte

But the brief relationship did not last.

May 4th Motored for the day to Fontainebleau with Ralph Lambton and Lord Cochran. On the way down we passed Lord Derby and Lady Wolverton stuck on the road with a puncture!
   When we arrived the men played golf and Joan and I walked in the gardens of the Chateau. Don't care much for Lord Cochran, who is very dull and conceited. Dined with Ralph and Col. Geoffrey Glyn and went to see a play, *Les Soeurs d'Amour* with Comte and Comtesse Berthier and Mrs. Paget. Play well acted but with an unpleasant plot. Supper at Ritz after.

May 5th Left for London this morning. Rene saw us off at the Gare du Nord. Met Victor Churchill at Boulogne with whom we travelled back. I had a row with him. He made me feel very angry and caused ill feeling with Joan. Feel depressed tonight. Last part of the journey was spoiled by all this.

*

Lord Churchill, another man of influence who was seemingly taken with Sarah and did a great deal for her at this time, was twenty-seven years her senior. Nevertheless, from this cryptic account of a cross-Channel journey with him and Joan Mulholland, it can only be supposed that Lord Churchill may have annoyed Sarah by paying her too much attention and not enough to her friend. Evidently no harm was done, for Churchill continues to feature in the diaries.

May 7th Motored to Cambridge for the day with Gail and Mrs. Alexander. Had lunch with two American officers up there taking a course. There are two hundred of them. The idea is for good feeling between our countries. Joey dined with me tonight and told me he was in love with me. It came as a surprise.

May 9th Took the boys shopping this morning for boots. At 4.30 Joey came to pick me up and we met Claud and Joan at the station and all went down to Maitlands house, 'Kyson' at Woodbridge for the weekend. How the Mrs Grundys would talk, if they knew! We had a wonderful dinner and walked in the moonlight until late.

May 10th Glorious day. Got up rather late. Joey and I are together most of the time, leaving Joan and Claud, for whom we are endeavouring to make a match. Joey and I walked up on the downs, a lovely spot, where he asked me to marry him. I am very fond of him but feel I can never care for any of these men enough to marry them. Wish I could but it is hopeless.

May 12th Joey dined with me tonight. There is something about him that attracts me.

May 14th Shopped in morning. Olive Pike came to lunch and Joey took me and Betty to the Zoo in the afternoon. Had tea with Eva Anstruther and went to Opera tonight with Pedro de Zulueta, Joan and the Marquis d'Argnois to see *Thais*. Louise Edvina was singing. She was quite magnificent. Supper afterwards at the Zuluetas' flat.

May 15th Lunched with Joey at Hyde Park Hotel. Spent afternoon with Freddy, we sat in the park. Oh, what a life! Dined with B-W's and went to bed early.

May 16th Lunched with Col. Mostyn-Owen at Ritz. He is back from France. Met Joey afterwards. Freddy brought his children, Basil and Veronica, to tea today. They are charming and have such nice manners. Went to opera with Joey to see Louise singing *Tosca*. Enjoyed it. She is a wonderful actress but her voice is too small for Covent Garden.

May 17th Joey motored me down to Bognor to stay the weekend with Sir Arthur du Cros. We had a puncture, which delayed us for two hours. Sir Arthur asked Joey to stay over the weekend. How we have laughed over this!

May 24th Went to Estelle, the Palmist. Had my hair washed and lunched in. The Duke of Connaught came in to see me at 3.30 and stayed until 4.45. He is sending me tickets for the Trooping of the Colour and for Ascot. Dined with Joey and we went to see *Madame Butterfly* at Opera.

May 25th Cloudy day. Claud, Joey and Joan called for me and we all went down to the Guards Boat Club at Maidenhead. Happy day on the river.

May 26th Robin Cooper [a young American friend from Nashville] is in London on his way to Paris. He lunched here and I loved hearing all the home news. We walked in the park and he proposed to me. I could never marry him.

May 27th Lunched at Duchess of Abercorn's and met her daughter, Lady Mary Kenyon-Slaney. She is very attractive. Claud was there. Afterwards Joey motored me to Hampton Court.

May 29th Received most upsetting letter from Lord Shaughnessy. It has made me miserable. I've simply lost heart in my trip to Canada. [She was due to take her three children over later that summer.] Dined in alone. Very depressed.

June 4th Cameron of Lochiel, Hermione, Mr and Mrs Geoffrey Howard [of Castle Howard] and Claud came to lunch with me. Tonight I dined with Freddy and Brenda and went on in a party to the Russian Ballet. Then on to Mrs. Peto's small dance. Band never turned up, so party didn't last long. Freddy brought me home.

June 5th Lunched at Clarence House with Duke of Connaught. Lady Patricia and Cmdr. Ramsay there, also Sir Douglas and Lady Haig, Sir Henry and Lady Rawlinson, Lord and Lady St. Levan. Joey fetched me afterwards.

In early June Joey Legh went off somewhere for a week with the Prince of Wales. Meanwhile Sarah's social life proceeded as usual.

June 6th Lunched with Eddie. Met children in Hyde Park at 3.30. Freddy brought Veronica and we all had tea in the park. Freddy and I motored out to Tagg's Island for dinner. It was lovely on the river.

June 7th Went to Ranelagh to watch the polo. Claud came to dine with me.

June 10th Louise Edvina gave me a box at the Opera, so I asked a party to hear *Manon*.

June 12th Joey has returned and came here to dine. I am so glad to see him again.

June 17th Joey and I went to Ascot, opening day. Lunched with Victor Churchill in his private box and he was very kind. Afterwards we walked about and chatted with various friends, including the P.O.W. and Prince Albert [later George VI]. Dined with Freddy and went to the Russian Ballet.

Royal Ascot now being over, Sarah and Joan went off to Paris to stay with the tall and elegant Ralph Lambton, principally for the signing of the Peace Treaty at Versailles. Being lent a motor car and chauffeur by her kind admirer and host, Sarah took the opportunity to call on her unmarried cousin, Miss Rebecca Polk, from her mother's side of the family, who now lived quietly with a friend, Miss Henderson, in a small flat in I believe the avenue Émile d'Eschads. Sarah also saw, as usual in Paris, her old flame, Réné Escudier, who had met and fallen for her when she was a young girl in Paris in 1910. She also attended the races at Auteuil; went with Rex Benson and some French people to see a play called *La bonheur de ma femme* which Sarah described as 'leaving nothing to the imagination'; and indulged in some shopping with Joan. On the night of the 23rd Ralph Lambton gave a dinner-party and dance at his sumptuous flat and invited the cream of Paris society, as well as some visiting English people, including Capt. and Lady Victoria Bullock, Lord Pembroke and a Mrs Chichester. Major R. [Rex] Benson and two Americans made up the band. Sarah records: 'They were disguised as U.S. sailors and played awfully well. The dance was a great success.'

June 26th Joan and I lunched with Mr. Chichester at his flat. Ralph came for us and we motored out to Versailles to the Trianon, where Major Curry gave us a permit to see the Galeries de Glaces [Hall of Mirrors] where Peace is to be signed.

June 27th Played tennis this morning at Tir aux Pigeons in the Bois with Rene Escudier, Comte de Rougemont and the Princess de la Tourdogne. Lunched in and went to Auteuil races with Sir Samuel Scott and had tea there with Lord Charles Montagu. Dined at the Ritz with Mr. Baruch, Head of the American Mission. Others there were the Prince de Broglie, Comte de Rougemont, Madame de Wendel, Col. Glyn and others. We danced afterwards. Joey arrived in Paris tonight for the Grand Prix. Was so glad to see him.

June 28th Peace signed today at Versailles. Lunched early and Ralph, Joan and I motored out to Versailles to witness the Peace celebrations. Sir Percy Loraine gave us tickets to the gardens in front of the Palais. After the Germans had signed, guns were fired but the crowd was calm. It was a most thrilling experience. We saw President Wilson, Clemenceau and Lloyd George walk through the crowd in the gardens, being cheered, and all the fountains began to play. Major Curry came to dine and we went on afterwards to the Majestic to a ball, which wasn't much fun.

June 29th Went out this morning with Joey to see my cousin, Miss Rebecca Polk. Lunched with Comtesse de Breselan in a big party, then on to Longchamps for the Grand Prix, where I backed 'Galloper Light', which won. Ralph had a dinner party tonight, Prince and Princess Caramon de Chimay, Sir Percy Loraine, Capt. and Mrs Mackenzie, Sir Esme and Lady Howard, Mrs. Chichester, Mr and Mrs Graves, Joey, Joan and me. About twenty people came in to dance afterwards. It was great fun.

June 30th Returned to London. Most terrible crossing, everybody was sick. Joey came with us. Never again will I travel *en trois* like that. It's the limit.

July 1st Stayed in bed most of day. Joey came to tea. He is very busy with the Prince this month. Dined in alone and wrote letters to the Shaughnessys. Very difficult it was too, when they have hurt me so much. I try so hard but sometimes I believe there is no pleasing them.

July 3rd Lunched with Joey at the Ritz. We took Tommy and Freddy to the zoo in the afternoon.

July 10th Joan and Lady Mary Kenyon-Slaney came to tea. Motored down to Syon House with Lady Newton [Joey's mother] to the Duchess of Northumberland's ball. Wonderful house and lovely ball. Most of the Royalties were there. King and Queen of Portugal but not the Prince of Wales, he doesn't go now on account of Mrs. D-W. [Dudley Ward]. Got home at 4.30.

July 15th Went today to see about my passage to Canada on Aug. 2nd. All boats are delayed on account of strikes. Dufferins came to lunch, also Ralph Lambton and Ethel McGibbon. Gen. Townshend didn't turn up.

On 16 July, the day after the Dufferins had lunched at Sussex Gardens, Sarah received this letter:

Carlton Club, Pall Mall
Aug. 15th

My Dear Darling,

The sun is not shining today. You may have thought that was the old fraud you saw this morning but it just wasn't. I had no luck this morning. There were quite a lot of people in the park, who had the devilish impertinence to look quite like you at a distance, and my indignation, when on closer inspection I found they were some perfectly uninteresting females just cumbering the world, was quite pathetic. However I only had a hope you might come, you said you probably couldn't . . . I feel I don't really care about anything, as long as you let me love you. If I lost you, then I simply couldn't carry on. You have entwined yourself so absolutely around my heart and I just love you with all the power and strength that is in me. I am going to the Christian Science church on Sunday. Shall I see you? It would be darling of you, if you came.

Yr loving Freddy.

June 17th Lunched with Northcliffes and met there Sir Arthur Stanley, Gen. Lambton, Sir H. Hudson, Lord Knutsford, Lord Montagu. It was all very political and very interesting. Met Joey afterwards. Dined with Victor Churchill and went to the Russian Ballet.

June 19th Peace Day. Claud fetched me and Betty and took us to the Royal Enclosure at Buckingham Palace to see the Peace Procession, which took two hours to pass. It was a wonderful sight. Joey came back to lunch with me at 3.30. After dinner we went out into Hyde Park to see the Fireworks.

July 23rd Olive Pike came to lunch. Went shopping with Joey. We met the Prince and his brother, Prince George [later Duke of Kent], in Bond Street and had a chat. Dined with Freddy tonight.

July 27th Joey and I motored down to Swinley Forest to play golf. Lunched first. Whilst there, Mrs Dudley Ward telephoned and asked us to go over to tea with her and the Prince of Wales at her cottage at Windsor. There was no *gêne* or anything and we enjoyed the afternoon. She is so pretty and attractive, I think, and he is really a great dear, so natural and understanding. They seem so happy together. I can't but feel sorry for him.

July 28th I lunched with Louise Edvina, who said she had heard I was going to marry Joey. I wonder who has been talking.

July 29th Lunched alone with Joan and shopped afterwards. The Prince of Wales asked to dine here tonight with his lady love. Joey made the fourth. We dined at 8.30. The Prince brought his gramophone and we danced a bit afterwards. It was a most delightful evening and we all enjoyed ourselves. They stayed until 12.0. 'The Boy' has great charm and personality. He seems very young but there isn't much he doesn't know.

July 30th I dined with Freddy at Claridge's, a goodbye dinner, as I am off soon to Canada. We came back here afterwards. Freddy is very depressed but feels, on the other hand, slightly cheered up as his speech in the House of Lords on the Douglas-Pennant case was a success.

In July 1919 there was public controversy over the threatened dismissal on the grounds of misconduct of the Hon. Violet Douglas-Pennant from her post as Commandant of the Women's Air Force. Lord Dufferin took up her cause during a debate on the subject in the House of Lords.

July 31st Joey came to lunch and we motored out to play golf at Coombe [Coomb] Hill. It was really too hot and I got cross, because Joey lost the way and we were late arriving. We dined out and came home early. The 5th is drawing very near. I feel I shall miss him very much and wonder if this separation, when I'm in Canada, will make me decide what to do. I am an odd creature.

Aug. 1st Went to tea with Joan to meet Mrs Dudley Ward. Joey came to dinner. Very happy evening, our ship, the *Baltic*, was to have sailed today but is delayed by the strike until 8th.

Aug. 2nd Lunched with Joey. Ralph Lambton called for me and we all went to Roehampton to play tennis. Ralph is a funny mixture, frightfully worldly and a snob but really very kind. Went to the Opera tonight with Lord Cromer, others there were the Duchess of Rutland, Lord Sandhurst, Joey, Claud and Joan.

Aug. 3rd Lovely day. Joey and I motored to Brighton, stopping for lunch at a little Inn with a pretty garden. I had my first lesson in driving a motor and simply love it. We had tea at Sir Sidney Greville's house at Hove and got back about 8. Joey stayed and dined.

Aug. 4th War started five years ago today. Joey and I feel very depressed. His last day before leaving for Canada and the USA with the Prince. Motored to Hatfield and had lunch in an awful Inn. I drove the car nearly all the way back. We dined at Claridge's and came back here afterwards. Well, I don't know why but I really believe I love Joey. I feel sad at this parting. We have had such happy times together.

Aug. 5th Such a depressing day. Heard the *Baltic* is delayed another week. I have to get out of Sussex Gardens by the 8th, as it is let, and have nowhere to take the children. What luck! I am disappointed how helpless we are. Joey sailed today from Portsmouth in HMS *Renown* with the Prince of Wales en route for Canada and the the USA. Dined in alone.

Aug. 7th Mr. Dresslehuys has agreed to let us stay on in the house until 13th. He was very nice. Had tea with Victor Churchill at the House of Lords. Dined with Gleichens. Sylvia asked me if I was going to marry Joey. We discussed it all but I told her nothing.

Aug. 9th Motored down to the country with Victor. We took a picnic and had tea in the pine woods. Dined with him tonight at the Hyde Park Hotel. I miss Joey more than I thought I would.

Aug. 10th Major Hunloke motored me, Joan and Victor down to Windsor for lunch and took us over the private apartments of the

Castle and St. George's Chapel. The band was playing outside on
the terrace and, for a joke, we danced in the King's sitting-room.
Just as well nobody came in. It was fun going wherever we liked.
We all dined at Tagg's Island, which was dull and full of dreadful
people.

Aug. 11th Busy day packing for Canada. Fearfully hot. Mrs
Dudley Ward came to tea with me and opened her heart to me
about the Prince and how unkind people are in gossiping. She
asked my advice about going to Canada and I advised her not to
go. I quite like her and feel sorry for them both.

Aug. 12th Busy arranging for journey. Dined with Sylvia
Gleichen. Sir Frederick Ponsonby was there.

Aug. 13th Joan, the children and I sailed this afternoon for
Canada in the *Baltic*. Victor Churchill took the children and me
to the station in his motor and was awfully kind. A CPR agent
travelled to Liverpool and did everything for us, seeing us
comfortably on board the ship and into our cabins.
   It is a relief to be really off after so many delays.

7

Canadian Interlude

Even at sea aboard the White Star Liner SS *Baltic* Sarah Shaughnessy's social life proceeded. Furthermore, she continued to attract admirers, as – not for the first time in her short life – she crossed the Atlantic in the company of her friend, Lady Joan Mulholland, to bring her children over to their Canadian grandparents for the summer vacation at St Andrews, New Brunswick. The odd coincidence – if coincidence it was – that had Joey Legh and Lord Claud Hamilton also at sea and headed for Canada aboard a British warship, HMS *Renown*, in the company of their royal master, HRH the Prince of Wales, cannot fail to conjure up an image of two widows of the Great War chasing their men across the ocean. Inevitably, it was not long before they all caught up with each other.

Aug. 14th Good weather. A Mr. Harold Smith came up on deck and introduced himself, said he knew Lord S. and had known Fred. The Captain sent down and asked us to sit at his table. There are four hundred Canadian and American soldiers and their English brides on board and a number of officers.

Aug. 15th Lovely weather. We have read, knitted and slept. Talked to Mr. Harold Smith, who is most interesting, widely travelled, a most cultivated man.

Aug. 16th Stormy. After dinner Major Whitemore, who was exercising his dog on deck, came up and talked. He is in the Canadian Army, very good-looking and attractive. He says he has been watching us for a few days. He has a sad face and looks as if he had some sorrow.

Aug. 17th Beautiful day. We met Lord Findlay, former Lord Chancellor, and Col. Lawrence and talked to them for a while. They then introduced us to Canon and Mrs Carnegie, who are perfectly charming. We seem to know so many people, it is difficult to be alone for long.

Aug. 18th We are in the vicinity of icebergs and going slowly. Talked to Major Whitemore for quite a long time. I find him most attractive and clever. A great reader and dreamer. Mrs Freddy Guest is on board. We have played tennis together and talked Christian Science.

Aug. 19th Tonight I talked to Major Whitemore again and he told me he was partially engaged to a girl in England and felt depressed about the situation. He opened his heart to me and told me everything, said he felt he could talk to me. What a funny world. How queer men are.

Aug. 20th Have seen Major Whitemore a lot today and tonight, to my great surprise, he told me he had fallen in love with me at first sight and had found in me what to his mind was lacking in the other girl. Oh dear, what a pity we ever met. More unhappiness ahead. We talked until a late hour.

Aug. 21st We arrived today at Halifax, Nova Scotia. Mr. Grout, a Canadian Pacific official, met us at the docks and we boarded Lord Shaughnessy's private railroad car, 'Killarney', to travel down in comfort to St. Andrews. I am dreading the meeting tomorrow with the Shaughnessys.

Aug. 22nd Arrived at St. Andrews this morning and were met at the station by Marguerite, Alice [Fred's two elder sisters] and Wyndham [Beauclerk, married to Alice]. Went on to the Fort to see Lady Shaughnessy, who welcomed us with open arms and enquired politely about Mother [Mrs Bradford]. I think she must feel very ashamed at the way she has behaved and is now very humble. Thank God all is well and we can be at peace instead of war.

Aug. 23rd Mother arrived here tonight from Nashville. So happy to see her. We have discussed at length the outrageous behaviour of the Shaughnessys and how they have crawled down. Have just heard of Robin Cooper's death. So sad.

Aug. 29th Bud and Rene arrived at the Fort today from Montreal, also Lord S. and Billy [Fred's brother]. They are odd people. Lady S. plainly shows her dislike of me.

Aug. 30th Have had a talk with Lord and Lady S. The latter tells me there is no room at Dorchester Street in Montreal for my children. I couldn't believe she could treat us so, after my effort to bring them over to see her. She is indifferent and acts as though she didn't want to see them. I've done the best I can and can do no more.

Aug. 31st Dull day. Lunched at the Fort, played tennis in the afternoon. Feel so depressed. This is the last time I shall bring the children over to see Lady S. She doesn't ask her own grandchildren to stay with her but lets them live in hotels!

Sept. 7th Left St. Andrews today for Montreal. Mother is staying on with the children until the 15th. Very glad to leave. Felt bored and depressed there.

Sept. 8th Arrived at the Ritz this morning. Joan is here. Agnes de Lotbiniere came up from New York to see me and we had a wonderful time talking. Admiral Kerr, Joan's uncle, is here and we all lunched together. Telephone has been ringing all day, old friends welcoming us back. Also newspaper reporters wanting Joan's photograph.

Sept. 9th Sir Charles Gordon lent us his car for the day and we drove out to lunch with Lady Clouston. Flora Guest was there. Afterwards we went down to Pointe Clair to pick up Uncle Mark to dine at the 'Trout and Stream' Club with Sir Charles. Those there were Orian, Miss McDougall, Lionel Guest, Johnny Dodge, Sir William Wiseman and Jack Todd. Very nice evening. Major Whitemore arrived in Montreal today and called me.

Sept. 10th The Shaughnessys are back in Montreal from St. Andrews. Joan and I went out this morning with Major Whitemore and we all lunched with Hartland at the Ritz. Drove in mountains later with Major Whitemore. He is the same as ever, told me again this afternoon that he loved me. Am sorry in a way, for it can never come to anything from my side. Dined at Dorchester Street. Lady S. very cold with me. Joan and I left tonight for Toronto.

Sept. 11th Spent the day at Niagara Falls, which is very wonderful to see, but the most tiring day I've ever spent. Not good enough, I don't think, to do too much.

Sept. 12th We have been bombarded by the newspaper reporters wanting our photos etc. Mrs Reynolds took us out in her motor round the city. I feel all the better for seeing her. We left for Banff tonight.

Sept. 13th and 14th On Train.

Sept. 15th At 9.30 am we stopped at Calgary and who should be at the station but Joey and Claud. [The Prince was visiting his Alberta ranch.] I was glad to see Joey, if only for 15 minutes. He is much fatter and looks better. Arrived in Banff in time for lunch, a glorious place. Mrs Hutchinson took us in her motor to the Golf Club for tea.

Sept. 16th Motored this afternoon to Johnson's Canyon. Feel bored waiting for tomorrow. Can't sleep since I've been in the mountains and feel very nervous.

Sept. 17th Mrs Hutchinson took us in her motor over to the station for the arrival in Banff of the Prince of Wales. We saw him in the distance, kept out of the reporters' way. We then went on to see the Indian display, where the P.O.W. was made an Indian

12 House party at Alnwick Castle, 1924. The group includes the Prince of Wales, seated between the Duke and Duchess of Northumberland, with the Duchess of Sutherland on the Duchess's left and the Duchess of Portland on the Duke's right. The second row includes Lord Grey (extreme left), Lord Esmé Gordon-Lennox (second left), Lady Dalkeith (fifth from right), Lady Hartington (fourth from right) and (third from right) Sarah Legh. Back row: Lord Dalkeith, Captain Allan Lascelles, Lord Hartington, Joey Legh, the Duke of Portland, Lord Alington and Admiral Sir Lionel Halsey.

13 Snapshot taken by Sarah at Trent Park, 1925. Left to right: Joey; Captain Aly Mackintosh, Mrs 'Poots' Frances (later Mrs Humphrey Butler), Freda Dudley Ward, the Prince of Wales, Lady Loughborough (later Lady Milbanke) and Sir Philip Sassoon.

14 Weekend party at Small Downs House, Sandwich, 1926. Sarah and the Duchess of York with the Duke of York, the Prince of Wales and Prince Henry.

15 Joey with his three Shaughnessy stepchildren, Betty, Tommy and Freddy, at Birchington-on-Sea, 1925.

16 Tragic weekend flight to Le Touquet, 1930. Left to right: Sir Edward Ward, Joey, Mrs Loeffler, Sarah, Viscountess Ednam and the Marquess of Dufferin and Ava.

Chief. After lunch the Prince sent for us on the terrace and we had a talk before we went off to golf. Before dinner he sent for me and I went up to his sitting room, where we had a long talk about Freda Dudley Ward.

Sept. 18th Lake Louise. The Prince asked us to come over here in his car but we thought it best not to. Joey and Claud came over in the train with us and we dined together. There was a dance tonight but not much fun. The Calgary girls, who followed the P.O.W. up to this point, are a funny lot. Met a Mrs Vanderbilt at the dance.

Sept. 19th The Prince sent for us in a private sitting room to say goodbye and then left with his whole staff at 10.30. [Apart from the two equerries, Joey Legh and Claud Hamilton, these were Commander Dudley North, Rear-Admiral Sir Lionel Halsey, Col. Grigg and the Private Secretary, Godfrey Thomas.] Joan and I both feel down and lonely. We took a walk in the rain and discussed Joey and Claud and the whole thing. If only I could make up my mind. I am hopeless. We rode on ponies up to the teahouse and were caught in a snowstorm. It was awfully nice.

Sept. 20th We left Lake Louise this morning, leaving our maids behind, and drove here [Emerald Lake] 8 miles, a perfect spot. Staying in a small hotel, just like a country house, so quiet and peaceful. I feel very near to God here, amidst this marvellous creation.

Sept. 21st Started off at 9.30 with our guide 'Charlie' to the Yoho. Not a cloud in the sky. Took the trail over the mountains into the Yoho Valley, to the high line at the Look Out, where we saw some huge waterfalls. Marvellous. We rode 14 miles, took our lunch by the Summit Lake and drove 18 miles back through the Valley and Field. I long to stay on here and do more expeditions.

Sept. 22nd Left Emerald Lake this morning for Victoria, British Columbia.

Sept. 23rd Joey and Claud met us at the Station at Vancouver en route. We arrived in Victoria this afternoon, after crossing from Vancouver by boat. This is a beautiful island and I feel I am going to like it best of any Western Canadian city. The Prince arrived this evening and is staying at Government House. Joey and Claud are staying in the hotel with the rest of the staff. We all dined together and went on to a dance for the Prince at Government House. It was great fun.

Sept. 24th Got up late. Lunched with Joan and Claud and played golf with Lady Barnard and two other women. Had a 'passage' with Joan. She was cross and moody and vented it on me and I got annoyed. Our first big row. Big ball for the Prince tonight at the Empress. It was a sight. All kinds and conditions of people. Danced a good deal with 'The Boy', who was getting bored with the crowd.

Sept. 25th Joey and I went shopping this morning. Lunched together and went for a long drive in the evening by motor. We all dined together and went to a dance. The Prince asked if he could come and lunch with Joey and me on Sunday and motor afterwards but I don't see how we can do this without the other two [Claud and Joan]. The dance was fun. Lovely house and garden.

Sept. 27th Went shopping alone, as Joey was on duty with the Prince but came back to lunch.
Claud, Joan, Joey and I dined together and went on to Government House to dance.

Sept. 28th The Prince came to lunch with us in a private dining-room. After lunch the Prince and I went out motoring. Crowds of people recognized him and cheered him. Poor boy, he is never left in peace. I shan't forget today and the difficult time arranging to be alone with him this afternoon! Dined with Joey alone tonight. The royal party left at 11.30. It has been a wonderful week.

Sept. 29th We left Victoria at 2.30 for Vancouver. Feeling frightfully tired.

Sept. 30th Terrible rainy day. We lunched with the Duke and Duchess of Sutherland and Mr. Dudley Ward in the hotel here and were taken afterwards by General Stuart to see the largest sawmill in the Western Hemisphere. Wonderfully interesting. We all had tea together, then Joan and I left early to catch our train to Winnipeg.

Back in Montreal, where she had lived with her husband for four years, Sarah caught up with many old friends and acquaintances, but the *froideur* she received from her in-laws, the Shaughnessys, continued to upset and puzzle her. She dined just once at Dorchester Street in a fairly large party and records that Lord Shaughnessy made an effort to be agreeable, while Lady Shaughnessy continued to be extremely cool and distant. Finally:

Oct. 13th Left with the children for Nashville today. I am so relieved to have them out of Montreal. The Shaughnessys have been perfect fiends and there are some things I can never forgive. Hard words said.

Having settled her three children with their other grandmother, Mrs Bradford, at Woodstock, Nashville, Sarah was soon back in Montreal again, staying with her devoted friend, Agnes de Lotbinière in Pine Avenue, close to the house where she had lived with Fred before the war.

Oct. 24th Received a long letter today from the Prince. Very amusing.

Oct. 27th The Prince of Wales and his staff arrived today in Montreal, staying at the Ritz. More than glad to see Joey, who came to dine tonight.

Oct. 28th The Prince came to tea and I introduced him to Agnes. Joey came with him and we had a nice talk.

Oct. 29th Joey and I motored after lunch. He was so blue about the future. I felt unhappy but things were better when we parted. I came very near to being angry with Joey this morning.

We went to Lady Davis's [wife of Sir Mortimer] dance after dinner at the Ritz last night. Danced a lot with the Prince. Rene asked me to try and get the P.O.W. to dance with Bud, as it would please her so much. Also Lord Queenborough asked if I could fix for his daughter, Olive, to be presented. I might have been an equerry myself!

Oct. 30th Joan and I decided not to go to the Civic Ball, as we were tired. So we stayed in. Joey was furious with me for not going to the ball and came up to the house at 11.0 pm, having stolen away from the Civic Ball. He spent half an hour with me and was in a peculiar mood.

What happened that night at Agnes de Lotbinière's house in Pine Avenue is also described by Joan Mulholland in her Diary and her version provides a possible clue to the cause of Joey's anger and 'blue mood' around that time. Joan wrote:

Oct. 30th . . . Joey and Admiral Halsey came at 6.30 then left, as they were on duty and had to go with the P.O.W. to the Civic Ball. Claud and Mr. Perry came to dinner. Mr. P. went on to the ball but Claud, who was not on duty, and I went downstairs to the little sitting-room, while the others stayed upstairs in the drawing room. However at 11.0 Claud and I were surprised to hear a motor drive up outside and someone opened the front door, came into the house and went upstairs. We looked out of the window and turned the lights off, so that nobody could see in. We could not see anyone inside the car, so we both sat and waited for three quarters of an hour, then we heard a noise of someone leaving the house and saw it was Joey!

He had evidently got away from the dance and come to see Sarah. We saw him pinning on his medals as he left. It was very thrilling waiting and watching. Claud and I quite expected to see the Prince arrive. The situation is altogether a very odd one, as the Prince is very *épris* with Sarah and dances with her most of the time. So the old cats ought to stop talking about me now. Claud and I are very interested and, if only 'it' would happen, it would be the most wonderful thing in the world and save the British Empire. We are going to try our best to bring it off, although, of course, there are two difficulties in the way – Mrs Dudley Ward and Joey! How curious life is, as Claud and I had hoped this would happened some time ago and I thought it might after I had introduced her to him at Joey's dance last April at his sister's [Lettice Waters's] house in Berkeley Square. The P. danced a good deal with her then. But now, of course, is a wonderful opportunity. There may not be anything in it but *nous verrons*. Claud stayed until quite late and went home in the pouring rain and would not take an umbrella.

One can't help reflecting on the fuss that the Prince caused seventeen years later when, as King, he decided to marry an American. Sarah might have proved marginally more suitable, for at least she was a widow and not a double divorcée. Furthermore she was the daughter-in-law of a British peer. The matter is, however, academic, as Joan Mulholland pointed out in her Diary. The Prince was already infatuated with Freda Dudley Ward and, had she been in Canada at the time, Joey would have had no cause for anxiety.

Nov. 1st Admiral Halsey asked Agnes, Alain, Joan and me to lunch in the Prince's suite today. Col. Grigg, whom I like very much, and Claud were there. This afternoon the Prince came up to the house on Pine Avenue for tea and tonight we dined with Lord Shaughnessy at the Mount Royal Club and went on to a dance at Dorchester Street, given by Billy. The whole house was illuminated with electric lights outside and vast comic decorations inside. I laughed a lot over this.

Nov. 3rd The Prince has gone on to Ottawa but Joey got leave to stay on here at Agnes's with me and will rejoin the royal party in Ottawa on the 5th. A happy, quiet day.

Nov. 4th Went down to Dorchester Street to say goodbye to the Shaughnessys before I go to New York. Agnes went with me. The reception was cold and distant and I broke down afterwards coming home. I've had so much to bear from them and I am glad to get away. Joey saw me off at the station to New York. This was the worst parting of them all. I felt miserable.

Nov. 5th Arrived in New York to stay with Lucy Rosen [daughter of Flora Guest] and her husband, Walter, who is an American, German Jew. This makes me resentful. I can't forget this fact. But they are most kind.

Joan came to dine and we went to a concert.

Nov. 7th Went out to dine and to the theatre with Lawrence Whitemore. He proposed to me again tonight but there is no possible chance. I can never marry him. He is good looking. That is his greatest asset. Agnes has arrived in New York. There is nobody quite like Agnes.

Nov. 12th Joey called me tonight from Washington, where the royal party has arrived to stay. He made me very unhappy. He has completely misunderstood all my plans and can't understand why I won't stay on here in New York to see him. But I must go down to Nashville to Mother and the children.

Nov. 13th Left New York today for Nashville.

Nov. 14th Arrived tonight at my home, Woodstock. Happy reunion with Mother and the children, my cousin, J.C. [Bradford], of whom I'm very fond and my maiden aunt Rebecca.

Nov. 15th The children are as happy as larks, they love it here. They are playing shops in the garden with a whole lot of old Confederate dollar bills that Mother has given them. Valueless, of course, since the Civil War.

Sarah and the children remained at Woodstock for Christmas 1919 but she sailed back with them to England in the new year to resume her life at Sussex Gardens in London. It is fairly certain that by this time she had told her mother that she had made up her mind to marry Joey Legh.

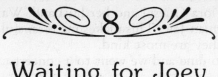

8

Waiting for Joey

The Prince of Wales and his staff, including Joey, had returned to London for Christmas in 1919, so that early in 1920 Joey and Sarah were seeing each other again regularly and, as an unofficially engaged couple, were receiving joint invitations to weekend house parties in the country. One such was spent with the Duke of Connaught at Bagshot Park, where they played tennis with the daughter of the house, Lady Patricia Ramsay, who had become very fond of Joey some years earlier during his time as ADC to her father when he was Governor-General of Canada. Accompanying Lady Patricia [popularly known as 'Princess Pat'] on her visit to her father was her new husband, Commander Alec Ramsay, and several other guests.

Another weekend party attended by Sarah and Joey in February 1920 took place at Trent Park near Barnet, home of the fabulously rich MP for Hythe, Sir Philip Sassoon, a bachelor and notable scion of the great Sassoon trading dynasty of oriental origins, who later became Under-Secretary of State for Air under Baldwin.

At both Trent Park (in later years to become a health farm) and at his other, constituency-based residence, Port Lympne in Kent, Philip Sassoon gathered the rich and famous under his roof until his death in 1939. Among those staying at Trent for a weekend in February 1920 with Sarah and Joey were the Prince of Wales and Freda Dudley Ward. Other guests were the Australian-born London society beauty, Sheila Loughborough (later Lady Milbanke); Mrs 'Poots' Frances, a sister of the great hostess, Lady Howard de Walden, who later married Prince George's Equerry, Major Humphrey Butler; and Captain Ali [Alistair] Mackintosh.

It was not long, however, before royal duties once again separated Sarah from Joey, for on 6 March 1920 the Prince was off again on a six-month royal tour that was to take him to Australia and New Zealand by way of Trinidad, the Panama Canal, San Diego in California and the Hawaiian and Fiji Islands, calling in at Bermuda on the way home. Once more the Prince and his staff sailed in HMS *Renown*. The ship had been somewhat refurbished since her last royal trip to Canada and a new addition to the Prince's party was his young cousin, Lord Louis Mountbatten.

Soon after they sailed from Portsmouth Sarah received her first of many letters from Joey.

> *At Sea*
> March 8th

. . . the departure from Victoria Station was awful. My family, consisting of two sisters, my mother and father, were all there but I hardly saw them, as just as we were due to start, I was told that the two Welsh Guards orderlies whom the Prince is taking with him, had not turned up at the station. So I had to find his car and send it off for them. They arrived all right – just as the train was about to start. Philip Sassoon arrived with Austen Chamberlain in the Rolls-Royce, which we both know so well, and I saw H.M. [King George V] eyeing Philip with marked disapproval. . . . When I finally got to my cabin, I found to my intense joy your sweet telegram, which was such a comfort . . . great improvements have been carried out in the ship. Wooden decks have been laid down and the cabins, including my own, have been considerably enlarged. The Dining Room and Sitting Room have both been redecorated but the upholstery is appalling. The cushions and chair covers are a bilious yellow, which is more than sufficient to finish off a far better sailor than I, if it gets rough! . . . a squash court has been built in the superstructure of the ship, which 'The Boy' [Prince of Wales] will no doubt patronize in the tropics. I never came nearer to breaking down than when we left Portsmouth harbour. Standing on the upper deck, I looked towards London and thought of all that I was leaving behind. According to custom the band played 'The Girl I Left Behind Me' which, in spite of its hackneyed sentiment, struck a deep chord in my heart. The Boy admitted to me afterwards that he also very nearly burst into tears . . . the new addition to our party, Mountbatten, is distinctly on the fresh side. He is very noisy and, although a good fellow at heart, is very young [twenty] and will have to be kept in his place.

By April *Renown* was well south of the Azores, through the Panama Canal, and about to cross the Equator.

At Sea
April 15th

. . . Tomorrow we go through the time-honoured custom of 'crossing the line'. The novices, who haven't crossed the Equator in a man-of-war before, are initiated by the orders of 'King Neptune'. As a prelude 'King Neptune' with his 'court' made his appearance over the fo'cstle after dinner amid flares and rockets and was given drinks to put him in a good temper.

We are all summoned to appear on the Quarter Deck at 9. am tomorrow morning. Grigg, who has been scoffing at the ceremony and laughing at the various messages and orders we novices have been receiving from King Neptune, is in for a bad time tomorrow, I'm sure. The heat has been awful all day. Damp, sweltering hot and oppressive.

At Sea
April 16th

. . . We were all on the Quarter Deck this morning at 9.am, according to orders, when Neptune and his daughter, Amphitrite (two Petty Officers) made their appearance to the accompaniment of a guard and band. Neptune was followed by his 'court' – among these Dudley North, responsible for initiating the novices. They were all very well got up. Neptune then invested The Boy with 'The Equatorial Bath', which consisted of an ashtray shaped like an ordinary ship's bath. The Admiral [Lionel Halsey] came next and received 'The Order of the Old Sea Dog'. Grigg and 'Dirty Dick' [Mountbatten] were then arrested and handcuffed on the charge of maligning King Neptune. All the speaking was done in poetry. A procession was then formed and we all solemly marched to the fo'cstle, where a large canvas bath had been rigged up. The initiation consisted of being placed in a chair and given pills consisting of soap and 'medicine', containing quinine and other ghastly quantities. The 'barber' then commenced operations with a large paint-brush. After one had been sufficiently smeared over with whitewash and red paint to prevent one from seeing anything at all, one was suddenly tilted over backwards into the bath to be ducked the entire length of the bath. As long as one was quite passive, all was well. But if anyone ventured to show any fight, he had an awful time. 'Dirty Dick' was nearly drowned. I'm sorry he wasn't! About 450 officers and men were initiated. You would have laughed to see the pompous Thorogood being mercilessly ducked in the bath.

Within a few days of crossing the line young Mountbatten's conduct on board *Renown* was really upsetting the Prince's staff. In his defence it has to be remembered that, as a young naval cadet at Osborne a few years earlier, Mountbatten had suffered deeply from the shame and humiliation meted out to his father, Prince Louis of Battenberg, when the latter was urged at the outbreak of war to relinquish his post as First Sea Lord owing to his German ancestry and to anglicize his name to the literal translation from the German: Mountbatten. Enough, one might think, to give any young man a complex and affect his behaviour.

At Sea
April 18th

. . . The inevitable storm, which has been brewing in consequence of Dirty Dick's behaviour burst in full force this morning. Grigg declared in his comically typical way that Dirty Dick must be left at Fiji (abandoned to the savages) to prevent him from further prejudicing the success of the tour. The 'Old Salt' [Admiral Halsey] gave D.D. a heart-to-heart talk and before he could gain the Prince's ear, the Admiral tackled the Boy about him. The Boy, who as I told you before, for some obscure reason likes the youth (I presume because Freda does) was entirely ignorant of how we all detest him. I think the row will have a very beneficial effect but nothing can really penetrate the hide of a true Hun!

This kind of blind racism was quite prevalent in the years following the Great War.

April 20th

. . . we arrive at Suva, the capital of Fiji, this afternoon at 4 pm . . . two correspondents on board are making themselves very objtionable. One, in particular, is an Australian, the *Times* representative. I think he is a complete Bolshie. He sent an article to one of the Australian papers saying that the Prince attended a dance at Honolulu (the Haiwaian dance) against the laws of the Australian Church. As a result shall find ourselves up against half the church in Australia . . . among the wireless messages we have received from other ships at sea was one from the *Baltic*, wishing us *bon voyage*. Wasn't that a funny coincidence?

Government House, Auckland, New Zealand
April 25th

. . . arrived here yesterday. Lovely harbour. As we came in, hundreds of motor boats swarmed round the ship like flies . . . Lord Liverpool and his staff met us and the Prince got a fine reception in the streets on the way here.

April 26th

. . . today being Anzac Day we had to attend two church services. The chief incident at the morning service was a dog, who ran into the church from the street and took a lively interest in the altar cloth, until he was seized and hurled into the choir, where he disappeared. The Archdeacon then preached a disjointed and uninteresting sermon mainly about poison gas! This afternoon's service at the Town Hall was packed. In the midst of a very harrowing service comic relief was provided by an officer of the Salvation Army who, in an address, recounted various salty anecdotes from the trenches, which at a Memorial Service for the dead struck me as somewhat out of place . . . our efforts to modify the programme here have been very much hampered by 'Liver' [The Governor-General, Lord Liverpool], a kind but stupid and inordinately pompous man, who invariably rubs the

Government up the wrong way. Massey, the Prime Minister, is a very strong Presbyterian and the story of the P.o.W. and the boilermaker's daughter at Panama has somehow reached his ears and he has hinted that any behaviour on the P's part of that nature would be strongly resented in New Zealand . . . he quoted the visit of Duke of Edinburgh [Queen Victoria's second son] who, when he was here, went off the rails with Marcus Beresford . . . the Boy does nothing but grouse . . . he hasn't made anything like the impression he did in Canada . . . of course Freda is at the bottom of the whole thing . . . he will continue like this until he gets a letter from her.

April 27th

. . . I am sorry to say the Boy took more than was good for him at dinner last night . . . a most unfortunate start to our tour of N.Z. Luckily I don't think anyone noticed and the 'Old Salt' has given him a talking to.

Throughout May the Prince toured New Zealand and various islands and finally set foot on Australian soil at Melbourne.

Government House, Melbourne
June 3rd

. . . we finish our official programme here on Sunday but, in consequence of the severe strain on the P.O.W. we are to have a week's rest here before going on to Sydney . . . with the idea of a holiday in front of him, the Boy has bucked up no end and has become a totally different person . . . he has done awfully well here and deserves all the credit he gets.

At this point Joey's longing to get home and marry Sarah manifests itself in another letter from Melbourne, in which he is mindful also, as a younger son, of the modest private means he could expect to supplement an equerry's salary, which was not over-generous.

Melbourne
June 9th

. . . I am on the point of sending you a cable asking your permission to announce our forthcoming marriage, whatever the circumstances may be . . . though we may be poor, sublime happiness is in store for us, which is worth all the riches in the world . . . my present income represents a total of £12 to 1500 a year . . . I have spoken about 'us' to my mother, as my father's financial situation places the whole of my future happiness in the balance. I have not attempted to disguise any of the love which I feel for you and have said that I must have a definite understanding of my father's obligations to me in the event of my marriage. They know that I wish to marry you, if you are so willing, as soon after my return home as possible. The trip to India is on so far but, with the unrest there, it may well be cancelled.

After a week or two in Melbourne, the Prince was evidently lapsing into his old ways again.

Government House, Melbourne
June 14th

. . . I was amused by your account of meeting Philip Sassoon in the dark and recognising him by the pin. There are many somewhat coarse stories about that pin, which you probably know already. I do not trust him a yard and he uses his influence with the Prime Minister [Bonar Law] very frequently in the wrong direction. Being a thorough sycophant, he merely acquiesces in everything the Boy wishes, whether it be for good or bad. There is still a strong movement, which I imagine emanates from Philip, to postpone the Indian tour. Personally, nothing would suit my book better. Honestly, I don't feel capable of undertaking another tour with the Boy in his present state, apart from anything else. The Colonial Office are very agitated and Wal Grigg talks of cutting out the whole of the West Indies tour in order to get back to England earlier and therefore give the Boy no justifiable excuse for postponing India. Honestly, darling, there are times when you would scarcely believe that the Boy is the same person we used to know. Sometimes, he becomes absolutely impossible, loses his temper and behaves like a naughty schoolboy. His selfishness becomes more apparent daily. A crisis was reached last night, when he lost his temper with the Admiral in front of a crowd of girls, because he didn't want to leave a dance, although he had promised faithfully to do so. If this goes on, I shall chuck the whole thing when we get home. There is a limit to one's endurance. Of course, the Admiral found a childish note of apology on his pillow next morning! We leave for Sydney on Sunday.

At Sea, en route for Albany, Western Australia
June 15th

. . . got your letter by the last mail which arrived yesterday. I was rather jealous as the Boy not only received three letters by it from Freda but he got your cable as well, which pleased him no end. I simply adored your letter and read it from cover to cover over and over again. I was delighted to hear from Claud that you had gone to see the old Duchess [Abercorn, Claud's mother] as I know how much she would appreciate it. I also heard from Freda that you and she were going down to Trent for the weekend. It must have been lovely down there in the Spring. I can't bear to think of it . . . by the way, something must have happened, as the Boy has had an appalling fit of depression since the arrival of the last mail and has been sending endless cables in code. He has rather given himself away by suddenly announcing that he doesn't care whether he stays on here an extra three months or goes to India etc. I have never seen him so upset before. No one enjoys his confidence but Mountbatten and I strongly suspect that 'Duddie' [William Dudley Ward, Freda's alienated husband] has been sent for and told the whole affair must stop. It's either that or he and Freda have been given some appointment abroad which they can't get out of. My curiosity is aroused . . . we are just half way through the tour and will soon be starting on our slow return journey . . . by the way Freda told me in her letter that your dresses and hats from Paris are frightfully 'chic' and that you look prettier and more attractive than ever. Darling, she is evidently very much attached to you, which is only natural, of course.

Government House, Sydney
June 20th

. . . we arrived here last Wednesday. It was a very beautiful sight coming into the harbour which, I suppose, with the possible exception of Rio is the finest in the world . . . the reception was just as wonderful as ever. Billy Hughes, the Prime Minister, who drove in the procession, amused me very much by suddenly taking off his top hat in the carriage and putting on a squash hat. A low political move to demonstrate his democratic principles. I was in a carriage with the Lord Mayor, a notorious Bolshie, who was received with loud jeers and booing. The Town Clerk, who was also in the carriage, kept on whispering asides in my ears. 'The Mayor is a Bolshevik, 'ark at the crowd', and then proceeding to say 'Are you quite comfortable, my Lord Mayor?' It was all very funny. As there is no house here for the Governor-General, we are staying with the Governor of New South Wales and Lady Davidson. They are an extraordinary couple. He is somewhat dippy, like the remainder of his staff here, and spends his time quarrelling with the Governor-General. The rivalry between here and Melbourne is amazing and their one object is to outdo Melbourne, if they possibly can. Of course they are all furious that the Prince spent an extra week in Melbourne and, in their childishness, the Sydney people say that it was only because the people of Melbourne behaved badly and tired the Prince out! . . . Claud is trying to have his usual adventure. He told me last night in confidence that he is taking a married woman out to dinner tomorrow night and asked me whether I thought it was all right, as the husband is away in Queensland. He is an amazing man, for he admitted to me that he thought you and Joan the two most attractive women in the world . . . Sheila [Loughborough] gave me some letters of introduction. I have met her father, whom [*sic*] Dudley North assures me was a doctor, although Freda wouldn't have it. He is a racing man, quite nice but has an appalling accent. I have also met Sheila's great friend, Molly Little, who is not at all *bien vue* by a lot of people in Sydney. So much so that there was a great 'to-do' when the Boy said he wished her to be asked to the ball here. She wears very vulgar, low dresses for a girl (no back) and is rather pretty in a vulgar way. The

Boy, of course, likes her for sentimental reasons. . . . Mrs Verney, the wife of the Military Secretary in India, is here and she says that India at present isn't safe for the Prince to visit, so I pray we may not go there after all . . . there has been a terrible drought in this state which has lasted nearly a year. The county is absolutely dried up and millions of sheep have been lost . . . we spend the day tomorrow at Canberra, which is to be the future federal capital. There is nothing there and won't be for ages, as far as I can see, as the Commonwealth Government appear to be quite happy in Melbourne, in spite of the friction, which it causes in this place. The antagonism between the Federal and State Governments is terrific. This is having a most disastrous effect on the whole progress of the country. However, there is not the smallest doubt that this tour has brought about an amazing change throughout. Everyone will tell you that the whole attitude of the people has changed in the last few weeks . . . the effect produced is far greater than in Canada . . . one hears that this tour has brought Australia much nearer to the Empire than even the war did. People didn't realize the war here. They had food in abundance and no conscription. If a man was married, it was a sufficient reason for him not to go.

At Sea
June 29th

. . . I have just been up on the bridge. It is blowing a full gale now and the waves are breaking right over the fo'cstle and throwing thousands of tons of water on the deck. It is an amazing sight, as the spray comes right up to the bridge, which is 90ft above the fo'cstle. Thank goodness we are in this immense ship, otherwise we couldn't go on but should have to lay to . . . the Boy still professes to be seasick and stays in his cabin with D.D.

Nobody knows the real cause of his depression but it's obvious something has gone wrong about Freda . . . your letters are the only thing that makes life endurable. I wonder how much of the champagne you have drunk. Mind you keep some to celebrate our w . . . . . g announcement. I wonder how you kept the secret of the necklace. I hope you do wear it. Does Joan ask any questions about the bracelet and what about yr mother?

A hastily scribbled letter to Sarah from Perth, Western Australia, was intended to put her mind at rest over reports in the British press of the heir to the throne's involvement in a rail crash.

> *Government House, Perth*
> July 7th

. . . just to let you know that no one is any the worse for the railway accident. In point of fact, I did not go on the trip and stayed behind here. I am sorry now, as they had an amazing experience. Only Grigg, Godfrey and self stayed behind. The others had a most providential escape, as the Prince's car and one next to it turned completely over. The situation was saved by a cow on the line, as the train had to pull up and was going quite slowly, when it left the rails. How nobody got pinned in the wreckage and why the train didn't catch fire, God only knows. They are none the worse but for a few minor bruises. You will see from the photographs in the newspapers at home how lucky they were . . . we leave tomorrow for Kalgoorlie, the gold district, then on to Adelaide . . . I hear we are to get six clear weeks before India – there's a great deal to do in that time but it has got to be done.

HMS *Renown* finally brought the Prince and his party back through the Panama Canal via the West Indies to Portsmouth, which she reached on 10 September 1920.

9

Courtier's Wife

The marriage of Sarah Shaughnessy and Joey Legh finally took place on 15 November 1920 at St Peter's Church, Eaton Square, a stone's throw from 75 Eaton Square, the London residence of Joey's parents, Lord and Lady Newton. Sarah's three children attended, aged seven, six and four respectively. They sat, all primped up, in the front row but one on the bride's side of the church. When two men in tail coats arrived down the aisle at the last moment and sat in front of the children, obscuring their view of the proceedings, the two boys muttered to each other with some resentment, until Betty, aged seven, whispered in awe to her brothers that one of the two men in front of them was the Prince of Wales, though she failed to identify the other as Lord Louis Mountbatten. So for all the staff's disapproval of Mountbatten's behaviour on the royal tour, 'Dirty Dick' did grace Joey's wedding in the company of his cousin.

The *Tatler* correspondent wrote:

Of course *everyone* was at the Piers Legh–Shaughnessy wedding last week, though there was of course the double attraction that the Prince of Wales was there, accompanied by Lord Louis Mountbatten, the Duke of York and Princess Mary. The bride wore a simply draped dress of mole-coloured crepe de Chine with a hat to correspond, the crown of velvet matching her gown and having a brim of gold and black lace. She carried a bouquet of mauve cattleyas.

Among others present were Mrs Dudley Ward, looking as attractive as usual, Sir Philip Sassoon, most marvellous and accommodating of secretaries, the Earl of Cromer, Lord

Queenborough, the Earl of Clanwilliam, the Dowager Duchess of Abercorn, the Marquess and Marchioness of Dufferin and Ava, Viscountess Northcliffe, the Dowager Lady Penrhyn and many others.

The bride's three children were also present. Little Miss Betty Shaughnessy in a bright yellow overcoat and velvet picture bonnet was with her two brothers, Master Tommy and Master Freddy, the former being heir presumptive to the Shaughnessy barony.

After the ceremony a reception was held at Captain and Mrs Legh's new house in Norfolk Square, W2, even nearer to Paddington Station than Sarah's old house in Sussex Gardens. 43 Norfolk Square was to be the Leghs' home for the next sixteen years.

The honeymoon was spent at Lyme Park, the Legh family's fine country seat in Cheshire, where Joey had grown up as a child, after which the couple set up their new home in Paddington and engaged a staff of servants – butler, cook, kitchen-maid, two housemaids and an odd man in addition to the nanny and Sarah's faithful lady's maid, Trott.

The Piers Leghs spent Christmas 1920 in London with the children and, early in the new year, Sarah received a gossipy letter from Lord Shaughnessy in Montreal which, to her relief, showed signs of a thaw in her relations with the family, while hinting at the old man's strong Catholic prejudice.

Windsor Street Station, Montreal
Jan. 5th 1921

My Dear Sarah,

Many thanks for the Christmas gift and please thank the children for their remembrances. I had a very nice letter from Major Legh, from which I gather you have now settled down to a contented and happy life. It can be no happier than I would wish.

Just now the chief topic of conversation here is the forthcoming Minto–Cook wedding. It is possible that there are some shoals ahead, because of the religious question. Lady Minto is convinced that difficulties have been removed but I have my doubts. In any event the cards are out for the ceremony at St. Patrick's but I have told Marguerite [his daughter], who is to be a bridesmaid, to be prepared for a transfer to St. George's. We are all well . . . etc.

The bridegroom concerned was the 5th Earl of Minto. His father, the 4th Earl, had been Governor-General of Canada from 1898 to 1904 and a close friend of Lord Shaughnessy.

The Prince's projected royal tour of India was, as expected, put back owing to political unrest out there. Even so Joey had precious little time to settle into his marriage with Sarah, for, in the late summer, the Colonial Office gave the all-clear and on 26 October 1921, less than a year after his wedding, Joey was off again with the Prince of Wales and his staff aboard HMS *Renown*, this time headed for Suez, Aden, India and Japan. This meant another nine months away from home and Sarah Legh became, not for the last time, a sort of royal grass widow.

The following Christmas of 1922 Sarah received from Lord Shaughnessy a warm letter which confirmed the old man's personal affection for her, whatever his wife's attitude might be. It was written on the threshold of the last year of the great man's life. He was becoming very blind and was to die in 1923, an event which saddened the whole dominion of Canada and caused all Canadian Pacific ships and hotels to fly their flags at half-mast and every CPR train to stop in its tracks for two minutes all over Canada.

905 Dorchester Street
Dec. 26th 1922

My dear Sarah,

I have received your very pretty and equally useful present of a gold pencil. Many thanks! Today I have written a brief line to each of the children and enclosed a £5 note to buy a present. To avoid jealousy and ill-feeling I am sending you £10 for the same purpose. I gather from their little holiday tokens that they are progressing as you would wish – a tribute to the care and intelligence of a kind and thoughtful mother. Our regular Christmas practice was put out of joint this year by sickness.

Alice's two little ones and Bud's daughter [other grandchildren] have the whooping cough and were therefore interned. So that we had a very quiet time. I was delighted to hear of Lady Joan's marriage and to such an outstanding and delightful man [Lord Cavan, a distinguished soldier].

Montreal is quiet as it always is at this season of the year – given over to dinner and bridge parties, more or less enjoyable. We have no plans at present but I hope to visit England in the Spring and see you all. With love to you and the children and kindest regards to Major Legh and with the best wishes to all for the New Year,

Yours Affectionately,
Shaughnessy

Over the next two years Sarah and Joey Legh's life followed a fairly routine pattern. When he was not actually 'in waiting', which meant working daily with the Prince in the office at York House, St James's Palace, his London home, or accompanying him on endless visits to barracks, hospitals, schools, town halls and factories, he and Sarah pursued a pretty busy social life.

Being well known as a good shot, Joey was invited with his wife to many shooting weekends in large country houses, while in London their life was an endless round of dinner-parties, dances, luncheons and race meetings, interspersed with visits to the opera, the theatre and, on occasions, the cinema. There were also frequent evenings out in London's West End dancing with the Prince and his circle at Ciro's, the Embassy, the Café de Paris and other night spots.

On 28 March 1924, Sarah gave birth to her fourth child, a daughter. Joey was overjoyed and the little Legh girl was named Diana Evelyn. She was duly christened at St Margaret's, Westminster, and among her godparents were the Prince of Wales; the Admiral of the Fleet, Earl Beatty; Viscountess Ednam, a half sister of the Duke of Sutherland and wife to Eric, later the Prince's close friend, the Earl of Dudley; and the Countess of Cavan, who was Sarah's oldest and closest friend, formerly Lady Joan Mulholland, now married to the distinguished general, who was by this time Chief of the Imperial General Staff.

The area north of Hyde Park, around Marble Arch, Paddington and Bayswater was in the mid-twenties about as fashionable a district to live in as are Kensington and Chelsea today. The twenties were also a time of the great London 'pea-souper' fogs, and an extract from Joan Cavan's diary, written a few months after Diana Legh's christening, illustrates the rather quaint conditions prevailing in London at the time.

Jan. 15th 1925

. . . K [Lady Cavan's nickname for her husband] and I dined with Honor and Becky [Colonel and Mrs Merton Beckwith-Smith] at 13, Sussex Square and went to see *A Kiss for Cinderella*. Norman McKinnell was the Policeman and Hilda Trevelyan was Cinderella.

When we came out of the theatre there was an awful fog and Becky had to walk in front of the motor most of the way home. Then a policeman loomed up in Park Lane and guided us across the Marble Arch but, at the beginning of the Bayswater Road, it was so thick we had to leave John [the Cavans' chauffeur] and the motor and walk. We left Becky and Honor to walk to Sussex Square. K and I walked with great difficulty up the Edgware Road and Bryanston Street to home [22 Great Cumberland Place, in the crescent]. Terribly thick. In the Edgware Road we met Aunt Cora [widow of the 4th Earl of Strafford] being escorted by her butler and chauffeur! She had been dining with Flora Guest in Connaught Square.

In 1925 the Prince was off yet again. With Joey and other members of his staff he left Portsmouth aboard HMS *Repulse* on 28 March, Diana Legh's first birthday, and once again the itinerary was a killer: a seven months' tour to take in the whole of Africa and South America.

Jagersfontein
May 24th

. . . what is very gratifying is the truly marvellous reception the Prince is getting here, not only from the English but from the Dutch as well. The farmers are coming in from hundreds of miles away, just to catch a glimpse of him. It's not surprising that great racial tension exists between the races, considering the Boer War only ended just over 20 years ago. It will be interesting to see how H.R.H. is received in the Orange Free State, when we go to Bloemfontein tomorrow . . . the 'Old Salt' had a nice letter from [Lord] Stamfordham [the King's Private Secretary] intimating that Buck House had approved our behaviour in West Africa, which is something to be thankful for . . . the P's craze for golf is continuing and I've just come in from giving him a lesson. He is improving but too impatient to be any good at it . . . the ukulele is going as hard as ever in the evenings in the train . . . he has become quite good and I must say it's an improvement on the drums . . . we had our first real native show last week at Umtata. One of the Chiefs, who made his speech in English, convulsed us with laughter by saying that the Prince of Wales had come down from Heaven at considerable inconvenience to see his children (meaning the natives) . . . the effect was rather spoilt by the Chiefs all being got up in European clothes instead of the usual variegated blankets for which they pay incredibly large prices. The women, when they are engaged to be married, and the boys, when they are circumcised at 16, have their faces painted white, presumably as a symbol of Purity. . . . I do hope Mary Kenyon-Slaney has seen you and given you the latest news of me. I told her she was to ring you up directly she got back . . . the P. had a cable last night from Clive Wigram announcing Fruity Metcalfe's engagement to Barbara [Lady Alexandra] Curzon . . . I must say I was dumbfounded by the news but I do admire her for sticking to him, in spite of all the opposition.

There is no doubt that Joey was torn, during these long absences abroad, between concern that Sarah should not get too bored or lonely and tinges of anxiety that she might overdo the social activity, knowing the sort of person she was. Sarah had written to him from Cimbrone, Ravello, the beautiful, now famous, Italian villa overlooking the Golfo di Salerno, which belonged to their close friends, Lord and Lady Grimthorpe.

During the long, hot lonely nights aboard *Repulse* Joey had also been thinking about purchasing a new car on his return to England. His ambition was to follow the current craze and get an American car – a Chrysler saloon.

Westminster
May 31st

. . . so glad to hear you are feeling so much better and stronger as a result of your stay with Polly and Ralph [Grimthorpe] at Cimbrone. However, I hope all the good and rest won't be neutralized by a hectic visit to Paris, where I feel sure Ralph [Lambton] will want to take you to every lighted candle . . . I sent you a cable two days ago but you are no doubt still at Ravello and haven't received it. I thought that, if we did decide to get a new car, we ought to do it immediately, as the McKenna Duties come into force on July 1st and American cars will increase in price. However, I shan't do anything until I hear from you on the subject . . . although the Orange Free State is Dutch and therefore anti-British, the visit to Bloemfontein was a great success. The Prince managed to create a wonderful impression that will do an immense amount of good. The nearest we came to a contretemps was when the P. decided to play a round of golf with the Bishop of Bloemfontein, as H.R.H. doesn't hesitate to use the strongest language whenever he makes a bad shot. However, though he played like nothing on earth, he exercised the most praiseworthy restraint and, barring a few mild 'damns' and 'blasts', there was nothing to which the Bish could take exception. I went with the P. to two very comic dances last evening. At the first, we arrived at the wrong entrance and found ourselves, amid roars of laughter and some consternation, in the Ladies Cloakroom.

We are having the usual trouble with the correspondents. The ones we brought out here are making a great deal of trouble by abusing this country to local people and generally finding fault with everything. Their chief grievance is that they are not travelling on the royal train but, as there isn't any room for them on it, their grouse is absolutely unreasonable. They have also been writing articles in the South African papers which have raised a storm of indignation . . . the Prince, the 'Old Salt' and Godfrey [Thomas] are staying at the Duke of Westminster's farm about two miles away. There seems to me something anomalous about H.R.H. being entertained by a man who is not received at Court.

*

By June the Prince of Wales was in the dominion of South Africa and Joey wrote to Sarah from Durban.

King's House, Durban
June 8th

. . . H.R.H. had a wonderful reception here, as Durban is very English . . . we went up to Zululand to a native show which was most spectacular. 40,000 Zulu warriors did a war dance that made the earth shake . . . when they charged right up to the dais on which we were sitting, one could imagine the feelings of the soldiers who fought against them in 1879.

Rand Club, Johannesburg
June 22nd

. . . in Pretoria we stayed at Government House with the Athlones. She is perfectly charming and so natural and easy to get on with. He is, of course, very German in his ways and inclined to bully his staff but he is not, at heart, such a bad old thing. Lady Maida Scott, Duke of Buccleuch's daughter, has arrived out here as a lady-in-waiting. She is awfully nice when you get to know her.

Bulawayo, Southern Rhodesia
June 29th

. . . Not since Canada have I spent such a hectic four days as we did in Pretoria. We were on the go stunting from nine in the morning until late at night, then the dancing began and, for three consecutive nights, we danced until about 5 am and at 6 am the Prince and I got up and rode with the Drag. The private dances were arranged by Ben Clifford and Abe Bailey's son, who made the best of the available female element, which was on a par with what we had already experienced in other parts of the country. However, I think H.R.H. enjoyed it and we all did our best to enter into the spirit of it all.

Government House, Livingstone, N. Rhodesia
July 12th

. . . I am trying to get some postcards of the Victoria Falls for the boys . . . I saw in *The Times* that you had dined with the Guinnesses. I think it was very pointed and rude of the Mountbattens not to ask the Lascelles to their party. By the way, I hear he (the Hun) is to be best man to Fruity. Tommy [Sir Alan Lascelles] wrote me a most amusing letter about them being married in the Chapel Royal and the reasons put forward by Lady Curzon to Cromer why the marriage should take place there. The Prince read me a letter written to him by Baba [Lady Alexandra Curzon] in which she expressed her delight at sanction having been given for the wedding to be held there. She said, although I don't believe this for a moment, that Fruity goes deadly pale at the mere mention of the word marriage and that she will literally have to drag him to the altar . . . the P. confided to me that he was very worried at not hearing from Freda, except for one letter some time ago, although he has written to her by nearly every mail. Hannah [Gubbay, cousin of and hostess to Philip Sassoon], who writes to him regularly, says that Michael Herbert [thought to be having an affair with Freda] has taken a cottage down at Sandwich, which may account for her silence. We both laughed a lot over Hannah's letter to him, which are full of scandal but also full of 'sob stuff' like, 'London is dead without you. I met the Duke of York last night. He was very nice but he isn't you and nothing is the same without you.' . . . the P. caused a mild upset by leaving the Civic dance at Bulawayo and going to a private one. He also rather shocked the Governor by taking up with a certain Mrs McLeod, whom I recognized as the former wife of Cmdr. Samson. We met her at Malta on our way out to India. Samson divorced her about two years ago on the grounds of her adultery with a midshipman in the *Iron Duke*, who is now her husband. Although they have only been married a year, they have four children, the oldest of whom is 5 years old! No wonder Samson got his divorce . . . the first thing I noticed walking into this room last night was an enlarged snapshot of my father walking with the late Lord Tweedmouth and Stanley, the Governor here, down to the House of Lords. Wasn't it curious? Lady Stanley is a young and very attractive Dutch lady from the Cape. I can already see that H.R.H. has designs on her but it will come to nothing, as she is happily married with a family of babies. Why she married this ugly old semitic man who, although he is very nice, must be at least twice her age, is beyond me. We have just returned from the Falls, a most magnificent sight.

Johannesburg
July 20th

. . . the P. hasn't had as much as a line from Freda, so I have induced him, for his own peace of mind, to write to 'Babs' [Freda's sister-in-law, Lady Godfrey-Faussett] and find out what is happening and whether his letters are reaching their destination. I haven't the slightest doubt that they are but the reason, I believe, is that Michael Herbert has such an influence over her that he won't allow her write. The P. confided to me that he had a desperate row with Michael just before we left as M. forbade Freda to go to a dinner at York House the night of the party given by Bridget [Lady Victor] Paget. He told me he wouldn't be surprised to hear of Freda running away with Michael Herbert. The only other piece of news he gave me was that Audrey [Audrey Coats, who later married the Chicago millionaire, Marshal(l) Field], who writes by every mail with the greatest regularity, has started a scent shop as a trial, so I guess she must be pretty hard up. Personally I don't think the P. cares two straws about her, except for purely physical reasons. The Gubbay family continue their correspondence. This time he received a letter from David, who told him Hannah was taking singing lessons – presumably with a view to serenading the P.O.W. on his return home. For some unaccountable reason the P. has no desire to return home at all and talked vaguely the other day about staying in the Argentine and sending the *Repulse* home. He wants to come back, as he put it himself, 'unofficially' in an ordinary liner. Of course the idea is quite ridiculous and won't be allowed for one minute.

After leaving South Africa *Repulse* set sail for South America by way of St Helena.

At Sea
Aug. 3rd

. . . we have been at sea four days now since leaving Cape Town
. . . we all feel better for the rest . . . I have written another play
for us to do, to amuse ourselves on board . . . the Admiral was
quite hurt, because there wasn't a part for him, so I've written
him in . . . the plot is very thin. The men in the play profess to be
confirmed women-haters, until the appearance of the only woman
in the vicinity (H.R.H., of course) when they all fall in love with
her in turn – only to find in the end that she has secretly married a
man they all detest. It sounds awfully silly but I think it will go
down alright. We shall probably do it on our way to Montevideo
. . . it will be interesting at St. Helena to see Napoleon's grave
where he was buried before they moved him to Paris and the
house, Longwood, where he dictated his extraordinary memoirs,
which I have just been reading . . . by the way the P. tells me that
we shall probably see Mme Thebaut at Montevideo. He hasn't
seen her with her hair shingled, so he will get a bit of a shock, I
expect. . . . I gave him a long lecture the other night and told him
he ought to marry as soon as possible, for he will never be happy
until he does find Miss Right. He agreed with me.

The tour of South America proved to be alternatively amusing,
comic and exhausting for the royal party, and extracts from three
letters Sarah received from Joey describing events in Uruguay,
Argentina and Chile pretty well sum up the rather limited success
of the Prince's visit to Latin America.

Montevideo
Aug. 17th

. . . directly we landed a huge mob broke through the police
cordon and swarmed round the Prince. Nobody seemed to be in
charge . . . the progress through the streets was like a pantomime
. . . the P. and the President had people jumping on the
footboards and the back of the royal car, shouting, gesticulating
and hurling flowers, while the streets were lined by the entire
Uruguayan army, whose uniforms were pure comic opera . . . we
danced every night until about 4.30 am, so am feeling jaded.

Buenos Aires
Aug. 21st

. . . again the crowds were colossal. Every window in each shop or house was crammed and the pavements were packed too. We were told that people had paid as much as £10 or £20 for a window place over the route . . . our hectic and sleepless life culminated last night when the P. gave a reception, followed by a dance, for 700 people . . . a success but a great deal of back chat from those who were not invited. It continued until the usual hour of 4.30 am and the only regrettable incident was when the Intendente (Mayor of B.A.) challenged the British Minister, Alston, to a duel for insulting his wife! However the affair was smoothed out and the duel will not take place. That horrible creature, [the Maharaja of] Kapurthala, has turned up here and managed to get asked to all the official functions – much to everyone's annoyance. We are trying to prevent him from following us to Chile . . . the British community are trying to boost up British concerns by making the Prince ride in trams etc and using him for commercial purposes. For this I blame Alston, the Minister, who though personally very nice, seems out of touch with life here and, as he is leaving soon, doesn't attempt to disguise his obvious dislike for everything in this country. One of the most glaring blunders he has made during the visit was to have a violent quarrel with the owner of the *Prensa*, the largest and most influential newspaper in the Argentine, which may well turn it against us . . . anonymous letters have been received from English, as well as Argentine people, saying the P. has not gone down here as well as he might have. The reason is only too obvious . . . he has looked bored to death most of the time and hasn't troubled to acknowledge the crowds . . . the one thing you must do in this country is to smile and look as though you were enjoying yourself . . . he says his depression is because he isn't allowed any recreation at all . . . he came here with the idea that he was going to have a wonderful time and it has been a rude shock . . . this – and the fact that he will *never* go to bed – is responsible for the failure of the visit and the Argentines realize it and resent it . . . he's had a sort of breakdown and we almost had to cancel Chile, as the doctor wouldn't take the responsibility. But he has pulled himself together now and we are going.

. . . we spent two very pleasant days on an estancia belonging to old Nelson, an uncle of the Duchess of Westminster. The old man came out here 40 years ago and made a pile out of land and ranching. He was very anti-British, prior to the Irish Settlement (1922), and was an ardent Sinn Feiner. His son, who manages the estancia, married a well-known Anglo-Argentine beauty called Miss MacDonald and was a member of the Argentine Polo Team that had such a successful tour of England in 1923. In spite of old Nelson's anti-British conduct, there was no adverse comment made about the Prince visiting them, and we were received with great charm and hospitality.

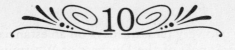

Grace and Favour

On 16 October 1925 Sarah finally welcomed her husband back, pretty well exhausted by an arduous tour, to his home in Norfolk Square, Paddington. Joey was delighted to be reunited with his wife and their daughter, Diana, now eighteen months old. The three older (Shaughnessy) children were by now at school, the two boys at preparatory school, Summer Fields, Oxford, and Betty at Miss Faunce's establishment for girls in nearby Queen's Gardens. There was no royal tour arranged for the year 1926, so Sarah and Joey resumed their normal life in London, punctuated by weekend visits to friends in the country.

Early in 1926, however, Sarah went off for a short trip to her beloved Paris, accompanied by her close friend and confidante, Agnes de Lotbinière, to see the spring collections, buy clothes and visit a few old friends. They evidently did not bother to make hotel reservations in advance, for Sarah wrote to Joey:

Hotel Lincoln, 24 rue Bayard, Paris
Feb. 4th 1926

Darling,
We had a very comfortable journey to Paris and a fairly good crossing, though poor Agnes did not find it so, as she was really sick but felt all the better afterwards. The Hotel Matignon was full but the Manager was very nice and found rooms at once for us here, a small, new hotel by the Rond Point and fairly reasonable . . . last night we went to see Mme Simone in *Le Lit Nuptial*, a wonderful play and very sad and tonight we saw the Guitrys [Sacha and his wife, Yvonne Printemps] in *Mozart*, the most

charming and delightful play I've seen in years. It is considered Guitry's masterpiece . . . we are going to dine at Ralph Lambton's next week but don't want to get too tied down with engagements and people.

Meanwhile Joey was pursuing his own social life in London, including a visit to a big fight. He was also in the process of changing butlers.

St James's Palace
Feb. 12th 1926

. . . the house [Norfolk Square] seems very deserted and quiet and I miss you more than I can say . . . I dined with Harry Preston [the boxing promoter and hotelier] at the Kit Cat club, an extraordinary party of conglomeration. Godfrey Thomas, Victor Churchill, the Greig brothers, Lord Decies and 'Baby' Colonna's husband were among the party. I sat between Castlerosse and Bertram Mills, the man who runs the Circus at Olympia. The Albert Hall was packed but the big fight was a frost, as one of the men was disqualified in the 4th round. . . . Baby [Diana] looks a picture of health and the family are all flourishing . . . I am dining at Eaton Square [with his parents] on Sunday night. I had to keep Saturday free, as the P. didn't know what he was doing. Now he is dining out and I shall probably have to pick him up late and go to a nightclub with him. He is in rotten form just now . . . I had a good reference about Lay [incoming butler/valet] from Guthrie and have told Blee [outgoing butler/valet] he will have to go on March 1st.

Oddly Joey's butler/valets possessed, to a man, monosyllabic surnames: Jones, Lay, Blee, Key, Rae and Eake. They served him from 1920 to 1945.

May 1926, of course, brought the General Strike and Joey, who enrolled as a special constable, accompanied the Prince of Wales round the streets of London at night, the latter disguised in false moustache and spectacles, the better to see for himself, un-recognized, exactly what was going on.

Later that year Sarah became unwell, although her ailment was never properly diagnosed. She complained of fatigue and depression and, as was so often the habit of well-to-do ladies in those days, she took herself off to a private clinic at Freiburg in the Black Forest of Germany, an establishment run by a Dr Martin. Agnes went out to join her there.

Meanwhile Joey's time was divided between royal duties with his master and, in Sarah's absence, coping with the children's holiday plans. These consisted of shipping them off to stay for the rest of July and part of August in a cottage at Ferring-on-Sea, Sussex, belonging to the ever helpful and kind-hearted Flora Guest, who became little short of a surrogate mother to them; then on to Gosford House, Aberlady, Midlothian, a mammoth pile rented by Joey's mother, Lady Newton, from Lord Wemyss during August and September, where she could entertain her numerous grandchildren.

43 Norfolk Square, W.2.
July 15th

. . . I trust that you are improving and that the swelling is subsiding . . . I haven't heard from Flora yet but I shall suggest that the boys and Betty go to her at the end of the month and remain down there until they go to Gosford . . . incidentally my Mother wants Lay to go up to Gosford next week to take over and I think I can arrange this, as I am moving into York House and can be looked after by the Footman there.

St James's Palace
July 27th

. . . I am sending Ruby [nurserymaid] and the kitchenmaid down to Ferring early tomorrow morning by train and motoring the children and Baby down after lunch. If Flora can manage, I shall keep them down there until Aug. 6th, then send them straight off to Gosford . . . the Prince wants me to go to Sandringham with him about Aug. 10th for two days. He is going to be alone there with the Queen and I gather that, if you are back by then, you will be asked to stay as well, as the P. says he wants some 'kindred spirits' there to cheer him up.

*

In July 1927 the Prince was off once again on a trip to Canada, this time as a guest of the Canadian Pacific aboard the liner *Empress of Australia* for the outward voyage and the *Empress of Scotland* for the return one. The Prince was accompanied on this trip by the Prime Minister, Stanley Baldwin, and his wife. Sarah received a letter from the ship.

Empress of Australia. At sea
July 23rd 1927

. . . I've been pacing the deck all afternoon. A very dull collection of passengers, as far as I can see. Mrs. Baldwin's hat is the one source of relief . . . Tom Burke, the singer, is on board. I think he rather fancies himself with the ladies but he is really quite nice . . . the P.M. has bucked up enormously since the voyage began and plays deck tennis etc. He is enjoying himself very much away from the cares of state. His party seem a nice lot without being exciting, the son, a serious minded young gentleman, who poses as a strong celibate . . . we arrive at Quebec tomorrow morning . . . spending the inside of a week on the ranch at Calgary, a week at Victoria and a week in the vicinity of Quebec and Montreal and we sail back Sept. 7th on the *Empress of Scotland*.

Canadian Pacific Royal Train
Aug. 9th

. . . we spent a hectic day in Toronto. Ancaster was staying at the hotel but, as he left for Ottawa that night and we were staying at Government House, I didn't have an opportunity of seeing him . . . after a church service we started the 100 mile drive to Niagara for the Peace Bridge ceremony, which in view of the Geneva Conference, nobody, including the Prime Minister, thought we ought to be attending . . . at Fort Eerie, on the Canadian end of the bridge, the Prince advanced to the centre of the bridge to meet the US Vice-President, Dawes, who had been waiting for us the best part of two hours in fear and trepidation of being blown sky high by sympathizers of the two ice-creamers, who are to be executed tomorrow [Sacco and Vanzetti]. The centre of the bridge was adorned by American and English flags and, as a symbol of the occasion, two stuffed seagulls, stuck on a pole,

fluttered ludicrously in the breeze. A piece of tape was then cut
and we proceeded across the bridge to the American side, where
the felicitations took place . . . everything went smoothly until
Dawes, who had purposely planned to speak last, delivered a
menacing speech on the Geneva Conference which, in the
presence of H.R.H. was not in the best of taste and is not
calculated to improve Anglo-American relations . . . we say
goodbye to the Baldwin party tomorrow at Calgary, a place which
brings back some very vivid memories for me [he and Sarah had
met there in 1919 during the Prince's previous Canadian tour] . . .
confidentially the P. has lost a lot of ground with serious-minded
people here who realize he only cares for pleasure and, in the
place of the young and attractive personality they saw in 1919,
they view him as dissipated and without a sense of responsibility.

Early in 1928 Sarah heard from her brother Thomas, who had
survived the war, spent a short time in Chicago and had now
taken up a new job in New York in the office of a big financier,
Roger Caldwell.

> *The Yale Club*
> *Vanderbilt Avenue and Forty-Fourth Street, N.Y.*
> Feb. 3rd 1928

. . . in my present position as an unmarried man, I can go about a
good deal and meet people . . . I met Lord Rothermere and a Mr.
Ward-Price, who said they knew you and your husband . . . they
are interested with a friend of mine in the Cuban National
Syndicate, which owns the racetrack, gambling concessions and a
smart real estate development in Havana. I have investigated the
stock thoroughly and I believe a small investment in it will pay
huge dividends . . . some of the wealthiest men in New York are
stockholders . . . Havana will become the Monte Carlo of
the West and big profits will accrue to the promoters . . .
Rothermere's group has purchased over 10,000 shares for
distribution in England.

Unfortunately Thomas, a well-meaning man, was unlucky in
business, and his genius for getting into dud projects left him

more or less bankrupt. A liking for the bottle ended his life prematurely.

In March Sarah had a recurrence of her old ailment, the feeling of jaded exhaustion, and went off once more in search of a diagnosis and cure, this time to consult a certain Dr Blum, who worked in the Civil Medical Hospital in Strasbourg. In fact Sarah's trouble was later diagnosed as thyroid deficiency, a condition of which the British medical profession appeared at that time to be somewhat lacking in knowledge.

43 Norfolk Square
March 17th

. . . I am so worried about you but I feel Blum must be an exceptional man and will be able to find out what really is the matter . . . I would give anything to get you strong and well again . . . the P. is riding in several point-to-points and is away at Melton for the weekend . . . I have been selected to go with Prince George to Glasgow in April. I don't quite know why!

On Dr Blum's advice Sarah's stay in Strasbourg was extended indefinitely and Joey began to wonder how long it would be before she could be sent home cured. But life had to go on and Joey began a search for his royal master which culminated a year later in the Prince's acquisition of Fort Belvedere at Virginia Water, his much-loved weekend home up until his abdication in 1936. Joey wrote:

43 Norfolk Square
April 20th

. . . I have been spending all today and yesterday house hunting, as the Prince says he now wants a house near London for the summer. As he won't have anything further away than Sunningdale, he might just as well remain in London and save himself a great deal of expense and others a lot of trouble. I saw four houses yesterday, including one Eve Bethell took at Sunningdale [Broom Hall]. Each one was more ghastly than the other and nothing under 30 guineas a week. Today I made an excursion to Worplesdon and saw a house on the golf links for

which 60 guineas were being asked. There was nothing to say for
it except that it was clean. No garden and overlooked from
everywhere . . . I am living in hopes that you will be on your way
home soon . . . if you really have to stay there much longer, I shall
come out to you at the end of the month, as soon as I finish my
waiting.

43 Norfolk Square
April 28th

. . . it is wonderful news that you will be home on Tuesday . . . I
do pray that the real cause has been discovered and that you are
receiving the proper treatment . . . one piece of bad luck. Freddy
has developed measles down at Ferring but there is no need to
worry. He is being well looked after . . . a doctor comes over from
Worthing whom [*sic*] Nannie says is quite excellent . . . the
others are well . . . Prince George really did most awfully well in
Glasgow . . . the visit was a huge success. [When Prince George,
as Duke of Kent, was killed in 1942 in an air crash in Scotland
during the war, Joey was given the grim task of travelling to the
site and bringing the Duke's body back to London by train for
burial.]

It was in the following September that the Prince decided to go
to East Africa on a big-game hunting trip and took Joey with him.
As a result Sarah planned to take her four children to the United
States to stay with her mother at Nashville for Christmas. The
two boys, Tommy and Freddy, were given special permission to
leave school a week early but to their bitter disappointment, the
trip was suddenly cancelled. King George V had become seriously
ill with bronchitis and the heir to the throne was forced to race
back to his father's bedside. As is well known, the King recovered
and went off to recuperate at Craigweil House, Bognor, the home
of Sarah's friend, Sir Arthur du Cros, where she and Joey had
stayed together before their marriage in 1920.

Sarah and Joey, in common with all their friends, suffered
mildly from the great financial crisis of 1929, which ended in the
forming of a coalition government under Ramsay MacDonald.
Joey lost some money in the Wall Street market crash but their

life-style was not seriously damaged other than the enforced cutting down of domestic staff. When people in high society in those days spoke of 'economising', it usually meant making do with one footman instead of two or giving up the under-gardener. Sarah, used all her life to a certain amount of luxury and comfort, continued to employ a lady's maid and to have her clothes made by private dressmakers. She rested on or in her bed every single day of her life for at least an hour, engaging the services of a masseuse, who came to the house every week, and thus, in spite of her chronic tendency towards inertia, somehow managed to withstand the social pressures of her daily life as a mother and a courtier's wife with comparative enjoyment. Throughout the late twenties and the thirties Sarah Legh found herself with Joey at endless weekend parties in all the great houses of England. Apart from visits to Sandringham and Balmoral, they stayed with the Rutlands at Belvoir and Haddon, the Northumberlands at Alnwick, the Sutherlands at Sutton Place and Dunrobin, the Ancasters at Grimsthorpe and Drummond Castle in Scotland, the Buccleuchs at Drumlanrig, the Angleseys at Plas Newydd and the Pembrokes at Wilton. There were shoots too at Lyme with Joey's brother and visits to Belton to stay with Lord Brownlow and his pretty wife, Kitty who, with her sister Jean Norton, was Joey's first cousin. They also spent innumerable golfing weekends with the Prince of Wales at Small Downs, his 'golf box' at Sandwich or at Middleton, Sunningdale, which served the same purpose.

Among their closest friends at this time were Admiral of the Fleet Earl Beatty and his American wife, Ethel, whose millions inherited from her father, Marshall Field, the Chicago store owner, kept the famous naval commander in luxury for the rest his life. The Beattys had four houses and a yacht. Apart from a London residence in Grosvenor Square, they owned a fairly grand hunting box called Dingley in the Fernie country of Leicestershire, a Scottish castle, Grantully, in Perthshire for the grouse shooting, and the Priory, Reigate, which could, with its proximity to Epsom, be called their racing box. But there was a price to pay for all this luxury and the Admiral paid it. As is widely known, Ethel Beatty was too rich not to be hopelessly spoilt, intolerant and plainly insecure. The handsome, bluff and hearty Admiral was a great ladies' man, pursued by women all his life, and Ethel, although smart and a good horsewoman to hounds, was no great beauty. As time wore on, she became more and more unpredictable and temperamental, given to jealousy, tantrums, rows, sulks, and appalling rudeness. All the same, in her calmer moments, she could be quite kind and thoughtful. But her mind was gradually becoming unstable and one passage in a letter from Joey to Sarah written from St Andrews, N.B. (North Britain) where the former was playing in the army golf championships, gives an idea of what Lord Beatty was going through at this time.

Rusack's Hotel, St. Andrews, Fife

. . . we shall have a tremendous match tomorrow against the Rifle Brigade. If we are beaten, I shall try to get back by the night train and arrive home on Saturday morning. If we are successful, it will have to be Sunday morning . . . what a pity there was no one else staying at the Priory last weekend. I can imagine how trying Ethel must have been for you, having her all on her own. I was much amused to hear about the Admiral's 'breakdown'. A put-up job, of course.

Curious to think of the hero of Jutland having to fake a nervous breakdown to get away from his neurotic wife for a spell.

Although Sarah and Joey were far from well off, Sarah did manage to achieve quite a reputation as one of the more smartly dressed women in London society. Photographs of her, taken at balls, first nights, race meetings and in restaurants frequently appeared in *The Tatler*, *Sketch*, *Bystander* and the gossip columns of the national dailies with notes about what she was wearing. The secret was that, after spending much of her youth in Paris, she had always taken an interest in clothes. Now, as a courtier's wife, she made a convenient arrangement with a well-known Parisian *maison de couture* called Paquin to wear items of their collections each season around London and at country house-parties for promotional reasons. Later, other dress houses lent her clothes for the same purpose and this enabled Sarah to go about looking pretty chic without parting with too much money.

In the summer of 1930 a shattering tragedy occurred, which must have scarred Sarah for the rest of her life, although she rarely spoke of it in the years that followed.

Towards the end of July that year she and Joey with a party of friends had decided to club together and charter an aircraft to fly them from Croydon to Le Touquet for a weekend of golf, gambling in the Casino and good food. Apart from Joey and Sarah the party consisted of Lady [Rosie] Ednam, Mrs Loeffler and two men who had both been deeply in love with Sarah in earlier days, Lord Dufferin and Eddie Ward, who had succeeded to the baronetcy on his father's death. The crew of the plane consisted of Captain Lockhart Henderson, a highly experienced pilot, and a flight engineer/navigator.

The flight out from Croydon across the Channel was a bit bumpy but the party landed safely at Berck Aerodrome and enjoyed a happy weekend at Le Touquet. On the Monday morning Sarah woke up in the hotel to hear a strong wind blowing and, being particularly nervous of flying, persuaded Joey to opt out of the return flight and take her back to England by sea from Boulogne. Warning her of a possibly rough crossing, Joey none the less agreed and the rest of the party took off by air from France, headed for Croydon.

What happened next remains to this day an unsolved mystery. All that is known is that around mid-afternoon there was an explosion in the sky over the Kent village of Meopham, near Maidstone, and wreckage of an aircraft, items of luggage and human bodies fell among the orchards of Kent and were scattered over a wide area. Everyone was killed, pilot, navigator, Lady Ednam, Eddie Ward, Lord Dufferin and Mrs Loeffler.

By the time Sarah and Joey reached Folkestone, the tragic 'society air crash' was making press headlines. Their friends were all dead but they themselves were safe.

Over the next few years, owing to the old King's frailty, the Prince found himself undertaking more and more of his father's monarchical duties, holding levees at St James's Palace, receiving the credentials of foreign ambassadors and so forth, while for relaxation he set about putting into working order his newly acquired weekend retreat, Fort Belvedere, at Virginia Water, near Sunningdale, Berkshire.

As frequent weekend guests at the Fort Sarah and Joey would be recruited after lunch, as were all the Prince's guests, for chopping, scything and clearing the undergrowth to extend the garden there, for the place had become HRH's obsession. On one such occasion in the summer of 1932, when Sarah was about to leave London with Joey for a weekend at the Fort, the Prince telephoned to suggest that her two sons at nearby Eton College might care to come over for the Sunday, if they could obtain leave. This was soon fixed and Prince George, who was also staying for the weekend, volunteered to drive over to Eton to collect the boys, delivering them at the Fort in time for lunch.

Tommy and Freddy duly waited beside the famous Burning Bush opposite Eton School Yard, dressed in their tails and top hats, for the black and red-lined Bentley they had been told to expect. The car drove up with the young, handsome and smiling Prince George at the wheel with a large Alsatian bitch called Dushka perched on the front seat. The future Duke of Kent told the boys to hop in the back and proceeded to drive them off at great speed over Windsor Bridge, up the High Street, past the Castle and into the Long Walk. Here Prince George accelerated and the Bentley literally tore up the Long Walk, raising the dust, up to the point, just short of the Copper Horse, where the main road crosses it. Here they turned off right towards Sunningdale and Virginia Water.

The two Eton boys, who were nervous anyway, arrived quite shaken in time to join the Fort house party for lunch. They were introduced to, among others, Molly Dalkeith, later Duchess of Buccleuch, Nora Lindsay, Humphrey Butler, equerry to Prince George, and his enchanting and amusing wife, Poots, whom they had already met at Chirk Castle with the Howard de Waldens, and a Mr and Mrs Ernest Simpson – she a ginny-voiced, smartly dressed, wisecracking American woman who reminded Freddy of the film star Rosalind Russell, he a quiet, modest Englishman wearing a moustache and a Household Brigade tie. Freddy's impression of the American woman was that she appeared to take charge at lunch and told the Prince to 'go sit down, Sir, and talk to your guests' while she took over carving the roast chicken on the sideboard. He remembers the Prince sitting down with a broad grin on his face and murmuring, 'Wallis can manage anything, y'know.' But neither of the two Eton boys realized on that summer afternoon in 1932 the full implications of the Simpson couple's presence at the Fort, though most of the other guests did. Things were already happening.

After lunch the two Etonians were much relieved not to be co-opted into helping clear the undergrowth. Instead Prince George and Humphrey Butler took them out on Virginia Water in a small outboard speedboat, where they roared around, having a great time and attracting the attention of the Sunday afternoon crowds on the opposite bank.

It was not until the following holidays that the boys learned from Sarah that the Prince was enamoured of Mrs Simpson but that 'It wouldn't come to anything. He'd had plenty of crushes on married women before and this was just another.'

Sarah was forty-five when, in 1936, King George V died and the Prince of Wales, newly become King Edward VIII, offered Joey a grace-and-favour house at St James's Palace as a reward, one presumes, for fifteen years of loyal service and friendship as his equerry. The house was at the corner of Pall Mall and Marlborough Gate, a large, elegant mansion with the back facing on to the Colour Court. It had been occupied previously by King George's Keeper of the Privy Purse, Lord Sysonby.

So 43 Norfolk Square was sold and the family, consisting of Sarah, Joey, Freddy and Diana, moved temporarily into a service flat in Victoria Mansions, Petty France, so that Sarah could be near enough to St James's Palace to supervise the decoration of her new home and the subsequent move. By this time her elder daughter, Betty, was married to Lord Grenfell and stationed with his regiment, the KRRC, in Northern Ireland, whilst her elder son, Tommy, had gone off to his native Montreal to read Law at McGill University.

It was from this same residence in St James's Palace that Sarah said goodbye to Joey on the historic night of 11 December that same year, when he left, on his forty-sixth birthday, to join the ex-King at Windsor, after the Abdication broadcast, to travel with him into exile. An article in the *Daily Mirror* that day had carried a photograph of Sarah with the headline *Parted by Husband's Exile with Duke*. The text read:

> In apartments in St. James's Palace into which she has scarcely finished moving, Mrs Piers Legh awaits further news of her husband, Col. The Hon. Piers Legh, who has gone into 'voluntary exile' with the Duke of Windsor. It may be months before she sees her husband again, as it is understood that he will remain with the Duke for some time. She has one daughter Diana, aged 12. She is herself an American, a daughter of the late Judge Bradford of Nashville, Tennessee. When she married Col. Piers Legh, she was a widow, her first husband, Capt. The Hon. Alfred Shaughnessy, having been killed in the war.

This perceived long-term abandonment of Sarah by Joey was probably inspired by a contributor to the *Evening Standard*'s Londoner's Diary who, the day before, had written:

> I predict that, like Lord Worcester and Lochiel in the days of the Stuarts, Col. Hon. Piers Legh will accompany the King into voluntary exile. The decision will surprise no one. 'Joey' Legh, as he is known to his friends, has been with King Edward ever since he came back from the war with a Croix de Guerre and two mentions in despatches. He was appointed an equerry in 1919 and accompanied the King on the various Empire and foreign tours, which His Majesty made as Prince of Wales. . . . Col. Piers Legh, who will be 46 tomorrow, is square-jawed, silent, slightly built and has a small cropped moustache. He is a more than useful golfer and a redoubtable opponent at poker. In both games he is helped by his natural characteristics. He is completely imperturbable and has an immobile countenance which betrays nothing. Incidentally it aids a natural dry fund of humour, which keeps his friends vastly amused. In this he resembles his father, Lord Newton, who with the same immobile expression succeeds in making even the House of Lords laugh. Both father and son are the kindest of men and big-hearted in their loyalty to their friends.

*

In the event Joey's dry sense of humour and loyalty to his exiled friend were strained to the limit of endurance over the next few months. But someone had to go with the Duke and Joey, typically, felt it was his duty to volunteer.

The two men had sailed together from Portsmouth harbour in a warship more than once before – aboard HMS *Renown* and HMS *Repulse* on the royal tours. But this trip across the Channel to Boulogne in the destroyer HMS *Fury* was a very different affair. The exiled monarch was in state of shock and incomprehension, which caused him to sit up all night in the wardroom going over and over the events of the previous days with Joey and the Keeper of the Privy Purse, Sir Ulick Alexander, who was also accompanying him. When those two courtiers had retired, exhausted, to their berths, the ex-King continued to converse with the skipper, Commander C.L. Howe. The latter later reported that the Duke of Windsor delivered to him that night a diatribe about 'my navy' and its need for more light cruisers and a stronger submarine force, as though the Duke could not quite grasp the unpalatable fact that he was no longer King of England and thus the Royal Navy was no longer his to discuss.

It was while Joey was in exile with the Prince at Schloss Enzesfeld, Austria, in January 1937, that Sarah received a letter from him telling her he was coming back to London to see the new King, George VI, who had asked him to join his staff. Joey had naturally accepted the invitation of the new sovereign, which he saw as a royal command. Thus began a new chapter in their lives.

Afterword

The new court of King George VI was of course a very different affair from the short-lived one of King Edward VIII. There was a marked return to traditional formality and stability. A higher moral tone predominated, and the Yorks were seen as a charming, close-knit family of mother, father and two young daughters. Confidence in the British monarchy was restored. At this time, too, the war-clouds were gathering over Europe and the country was becoming involved in a series of dangerous crises from Abyssinia to Munich, which culminated in the Second World War. The new King had allowed Joey and Sarah to remain in their grace-and-favour residence at St James's Palace and Sarah continued as before to entertain at St James's and pursue her social life, interspersed with work for charity. There were no more long absences for Joey on world tours, his duties with George VI up to and during the war consisting mainly of accompanying the King to royal functions up and down the country, as well as an occasional trip abroad to inspect the Forces.

In the early days of the war, as is well known, the Duke of Windsor was inclined to telephone Buckingham Palace at frequent intervals from his place of exile in a vain attempt to persuade his younger brother to get him a 'worthwhile job', such as Commander-in-Chief of the British Forces or Ambassador in Washington. It fell to Joey from time to time to intercept these calls, on which occasions he would find the Duke noticeably cool towards him, for he never forgave his old friend and equerry for – in his view – 'deserting' him after the Abdication. What possible use Joey could have been to the Windsors all those years in Paris was never stated. At any rate, whenever Joey informed the King that his brother was on the line again, he would meet with an irritated response, so Joey sometimes found himself playing pig-in-the-middle between the royal brothers, a role he did not relish. However, things quietened down when the Windsors were sent off to govern the Bahamas. Joey continued serving the King and Queen, being eventually appointed Master of the Household. In 1947 the King dubbed him 'Sir Piers' with a KCVO at a private ceremony inside Windsor Castle.

Since my own father had been killed two months before I was born and my mother had married Joey when I was four years old, my brother, sister and I not unnaturally grew up regarding Joey as virtually our father. He for his part took all the interest in us of a real father and shared with my mother concern for our health, education and general well-being throughout our lives. In some ways he was a very formal and correct man, totally discreet as a courtier should be. But in the privacy of his home and among his personal friends he was drily amusing, extremely witty and a marvellous raconteur.

By the time King George VI died and Princess Elizabeth had married and become Queen, Joey had been a courtier for over thirty years. In 1954 he informed the Queen of his intention to retire and make way for a younger man. The Marlborough Gate house at St James's Palace was now required for the new Lord Chamberlain, Lord Scarbrough, but as the royals traditionally never leave loyal members of their household homeless, Sarah and Joey were offered a charming little apartment in Kensington Palace and my mother started eagerly to plan for its decoration and subsequent occupation.

Alas, this switch of residence never took place. By the summer of 1955 Joey was seriously ill in King Edward VII's Hospital for Officers (Sister Agnes) with emphysema. This afflicted his already weak lungs and put a heavy strain on his heart. And Sarah, who had recently undergone a lung resection under the Welsh surgeon Price-Thomas, who had previously operated on the King, now developed cancer of the cerebellum and was slowly dying in her bed at St James's Palace.

On the day that Joey died in the nursing home, Sarah was lying alone at St James's, unaware that she had become a widow once again, for her children saw little point in needlessly upsetting her during her last hours. As she lay there listening to the chimes from the clock tower echoing round the Colour Court outside her window, she must have reflected on her long and varied life that had begun sixty-five years earlier and four thousand miles away across the Atlantic Ocean amid the cotton fields of Nashville, Tennessee, a life that was to end, within a few hours of Joey's, in a royal palace in the heart of London.

For the double funeral service that followed in the Chapel Royal, flowers and warm messages of condolence were received by Sarah's four children from the Queen and the Queen Mother. A large wreath was also received, with a somewhat formally worded message of sympathy from the Duke and Duchess of Windsor. Thus did the P respond to the death of his former equerry and friend, Joey, and of Sarah, his American wife.

Joey and Sarah were buried in the Legh family plot of the little church at Disley, close to Joey's old home, Lyme Park, in Cheshire.